Last Stage
to
Hell Junction

The Caleb York Western Series

The Legend of Caleb York

The Big Showdown

The Bloody Spur

Last Stage to Hell Junction

MICKEY SPILLANE
AND
MAX ALLAN COLLINS

Last Stage
to
Hell Junction

KENSINGTON BOOKS
www.kensingtonbooks.com

KENSINGTON BOOKS are published by

Kensington Publishing Corp.
119 West 40th Street
New York, NY 10018

All Kensington titles, imprints, and distributed lines are available at special quantity discounts for bulk purchases for sales promotion, premiums, fund-raising, educational, or institutional use.

Special book excerpts or customized printings can also be created to fit specific needs. For details, write or phone the office of the Kensington Special Sales Manager: Attn. Special Sales Department. Kensington Publishing Corp, 119 West 40th Street, New York, NY 10018. Phone: 1-800-221-2647.

Kensington and the K logo Reg. U.S. Pat. & TM Off.

Library of Congress Card Catalogue Number: 2018912556

ISBN-13: 978-1-4967-1677-4
ISBN-10: 1-4967-1677-9
First Kensington Hardcover Edition: June 2019

eISBN-13: 978-1-4967-1678-1
eISBN-10: 1-4967-1678-7
First Kensington Electronic Edition: June 2019

10 9 8 7 6 5 4 3 2 1

Printed in the United States of America

For Leonard Maltin,
who loves a good western

"I'll tell you what bravery really is.
Bravery is just determination
to do a job that you know has to be done."
—Audie Murphy

Can You Give Me Three?
An Introduction
Max Allan Collins

As a mystery writer lucky enough to become close friends with his hero—in my case, Mickey Spillane—I could never have imagined that the day would come when I'd be entrusted with his famous detective Mike Hammer and a number of other projects unrealized by the Mystery Writers of America Grand Master in his lifetime.

In 2006, Mickey called me and asked me if I would finish his latest—and projected as his last—Mike Hammer novel, *The Goliath Bone*. He was nearing the end of a draft, rather rushing through it to try to make a final deadline: he had pancreatic cancer and knew the end was near. I of course said I'd complete the book for him, but hoped it wouldn't be necessary.

This would be the last time we spoke, and I think we both knew it.

I said, "I love you, Mickey."

And he said, "I love you, buddy."

So began a great, bittersweet chapter in my writing life. In the few days remaining, Mickey instructed his wife Jane to gather up everything in his three offices at his South Carolina home and turn the manuscripts over to me.

"Max will know what to do," he said.

Over the dozen years that followed, I have completed (thus far) ten Mike Hammer novels, enough Hammer short stories to fill a collection, and two non-Hammer crime novels. For the centenary of Mickey's birth (2018), I edited his final completed novel, *The Last Stand*, and undertook to complete the very first Mike Hammer novel, *Killing Town* (begun in 1945, before *I, The Jury*).

And what does this have to do with a western called *Last Stage to Hell Junction*? Or a series of western novels about a legendary figure of Mickey's creation, called Caleb York?

Plenty, actually. While those books mentioned above may have been contemporary (if 1945, in the latter novel's case, might be called that), they were very much westerns. *The Last Stand* is a modern-day western about a flier downed in the desert and befriended by an American Indian. *Killing Town* has Mike Hammer, fresh from the war, coming to a corrupt city where one powerful man owns everything, and Hammer? He's a stranger in town. With a .45.

Mickey viewed Mike Hammer—and, for that matter, his other heroes—as a modern-day western hero. He often said that Hammer "wore the black hat, but he did the right thing." In 1961, *TV Guide* asked Spillane to comment on the increasing violence seen on television, and he responded by saying that impending violence led to suspense and constant wall-to-wall carnage resulted in boredom. With *Gunsmoke*, he said, the action "was about to happen every second and you knew it and wondered how it was going to come about." And if kids "wanted to emulate a hero," they got a good one in Marshal Dillon. "And brother," Mickey said, "you still don't mess around with Old Matt."

Privately, Mickey claimed to have had a creative hand in *Have Gun—Will Travel*, the popular 1957–1963 CBS TV series that starred Richard Boone. Mickey said he had pitched a "Hammer Out West" series, and certainly Paladin was a private eye of sorts. And one of Mickey's best pals in Hollywood was ex-cop (and future *Star Trek* creator) Gene Roddenberry, who was one of the chief writers on *Have Gun*. Asked if he'd ever pursued legal ramifications, Mickey just shrugged it off, saying, "That's Hollywood for you."

(A rodeo performer also claimed to have created the character of Paladin, right down to the business cards and the man-in-black persona. Some sources say Paladin's TV creators began the concept as a modern-day New York private eye—sound familiar?).

Going through stacks of unpublished, unfinished material from Mickey's multiple home offices, I also found three screenplays, among them "The Saga of Cali York." I'd heard Mickey talk about this numerous times—a project that he considered a major missed opportunity, rare for a man with few regrets. He had written the screenplay for his friend John Wayne.

In previous Caleb York introductions, I've gone into some detail about the friendship between Spillane and Wayne. But for our purposes here, let's just say it was a genuine meeting of two major pop-cultural figures in the early 1950s. Mickey starred in a film for his pal Duke, *Ring of Fear* (1954), and did a major, uncredited rewrite of its script, bailing Wayne out of a jam.

I thought the York screenplay was terrific. But it was

clearly not Mike Hammer, and it wasn't even a mystery, although the western yarn Mickey had spun had its crime elements. I put it aside with, "Maybe someday."

A few years ago, at a Bouchercon (the mystery fan convention), my wife, Barb, and I were having breakfast with Michaela Hamilton, our editor for the cozy Trash 'n' Treasures mysteries, each of which has the word *Antiques* in the title (*Antiques Wanted* has a western theme).

I was aware that Kensington was a major publisher of westerns and said offhandedly, "What if I told you I had an unproduced screenplay Mickey Spillane wrote for John Wayne?"

I knew Michaela was a Spillane fan, and figured she'd get a kick out of that.

She sat up and said, "Can you give me three?"

I choked on my orange juice. "Well . . . there's only one screenplay."

"We would want at least three. Could you develop three novels from the screenplay?"

The rest is history, albeit western-tinged. Mickey had created a rich backstory for Caleb (I dropped the "Cali" nickname) and a rather complete world in fictional Trinidad, New Mexico, populated by a fun, diverse cast of characters. With notes from him, as well as several variant versions of the screenplay, I set out to write not just a novelization of Mickey's screenplay, but two sequels.

And now here we are at Caleb York: Book Four.

With the exception of the novelization of the film version of *Maverick*, and a novel about old Wyatt Earp meeting young Al Capone (*Black Hats*), I had never pursued my love of westerns in my prose. I have read a lot of nonfiction about the West, enjoyed a smattering of western fiction, and been a hardcore fan of western movies and TV shows since my childhood. But writing a western would be something new.

So how do I prepare for a Caleb York novel?

Obviously I read a lot of historical material. Though I'm writing about the mythic West, I want an underpinning of reality. But for a month or so before I begin writing, and during the writing itself, my wife (also a western movie fan) and I mount a film festival in our living room. We are the only attendees.

For *The Legend of Caleb York*, we watched John Wayne movies, of course. For *The Big Showdown*, we viewed every western Randolph Scott ever made. For *The Bloody Spur*, we screened Joel McCrea's westerns. And for *Last Stage to Hell Junction*, we saddled up with a genuine American hero, Audie Murphy, who kindly provided our opening quotation.

You are free to cast Caleb York with any of these western stalwarts. Your budget will allow Clint Eastwood, as well—or James Garner or Gary Cooper or Burt Lancaster or . . .

Yourself.

Who's stopping you, amigo?

CHAPTER ONE

Friday night at the Victory Saloon in Trinidad, New Mexico, was a pleasant sort of chaos, payday always generating festive affairs at the tavern. Before Sheriff Caleb York cracked down, the whole town had been under more or less friendly siege every such weekend, merchants boarding up their windows and seldom leaving the safety of their domiciles.

These days, the sheriff—tin star tucked in a shirt pocket—could take the evening off. Right now he was sitting at a round, green-felt-topped table with a quartet of merchants, all of whom sat on the Citizens Committee, as well as at this table's weekend poker games.

The Victory remained the only watering hole in town, in part because Trinidad, with its population of three hundred or so, didn't require any more; but with all the ranches in the area, and for thirsty travelers on their way to Las Vegas, New Mexico, the Victory presented a palace where the customer was king.

From the towering embossed-steel ceiling hovered kerosene-lamp chandeliers, their flicker dancing off the gold-and-black-brocaded walls, saddles and spurs riding there as if deposited by bucking broncos. Those flames high above also reflected off the endless, highly polished oaken bar, in back of which ruled a quartet in white shirts and black bow ties.

Behind these bartenders—bottles of bourbon and rye lined up like soldiers ready to do their duty—mirrors made the chamber seem even bigger. Dusty cowhands hugged the bar, where towels dangled for patrons to wipe foam off mustaches; elbows rested on the counter supporting hefty mugs of beer, while one boot per customer hooked on a brass footrail punctuated by occasional spittoons.

Though tables for drinking men were clustered to the right as you pushed through the batwing doors, most of the cavernous enclosure was a casino, bustling with already well-juiced cowhands getting rid of their paychecks at dice, roulette, chuck-a-luck, and wheel-of-fortune stations. At the far end of the chamber, on a little platform, a piano player was providing lively rinky-tink noise for a tiny dance floor crowded with pairs of rough-hewn cowboys and silk-and-satin dance-hall gals, males and females paired off for some herky-jerky cavorting.

To one side of the tables where patrons sat drinking, and before the casino asserted itself, were a pair of gaming tables. House dealer Yancy Cole, a former riverboat gambler who still dressed in that manner, had a faro game going. The other table of York and four local city fathers was provided as a courtesy with no house dealer, or cut of the winnings going to the Victory. The pair of tables was positioned near the stairway that led up to the second-floor quarters of Rita Filley, owner and manager of the Victory.

Under the prior owners, one of whom was Rita's late sister Lola, the upstairs had been a brothel. But the sheriff had convinced Rita to restrict her girls to encouraging, by way of dancing and flirting, the purchase of drinks.

That wasn't to say that every fallen angel had gotten herself up, or that each soiled dove was, strictly speaking, clean now—but any girls with customers of their own serviced them elsewhere. A particular rooming house was home to nothing but girls who worked at the Victory— not exactly a brothel, as not all the girls entertained "male friends," and no madam was on the premises.

Caleb York knew human beings were flawed animals, and that certain things found intolerable by some needed to be tolerated by the rest.

Right now York was looking at three aces—also a deuce of clubs and a ten of diamonds, but those he would discard on the draw. Very good hand, particularly in this company, who were not as card-smart as the sheriff, who himself had a bit of a riverboat gambler look to him.

Like the Earp brothers, Bat Masterson, and other law officers of the 1880s, York dressed as a professional man—black coat, black pants snugged in black hand-tooled boots, shirt a light gray, string tie black. Even seated here, he kept on the black hat with a cavalry pinch and gray-knotted kerchief at his neck.

He wore his Colt Single Action Army .44 low on his right side, and usually kept it tied down—at the card table, though, he let it hang loose. A weapon falling to the floor and discharging could be taken the wrong way.

Big but lean, rawboned, firm-jawed, his hair reddish brown, York wore a full-face beard, though in the past he'd either been mustached or clean-shaven. He was squinting at his cards with those seldom-blinking, washed-out blue eyes, but truth be told, that squint was his normal expression.

As Friday-night rowdy as the Victory was, Trinidad

had been fairly peaceable, the big trouble lately a rabid dog he'd had to shoot—a canine one, for a change. January in New Mexico had been just cold enough—down around ten degrees some nights, edging no higher than forty degrees by day—to keep things quiet. That was how Sheriff Caleb York liked it; it was the winter chill that encouraged his beard, though he had the town barber keep it trimmed back.

After eight months or so in Trinidad, York was a well-established part of the little community. He'd rolled into town a stranger, on his way west to take a job with the Pinkertons in San Diego. He had been enjoying an anonymity from the false impression the world had that celebrated shootist Caleb York had met his match, gunned down in the street some months back.

With the age of forty looming, he'd decided being a live nobody was better than being a dead somebody.

And, anyway, he disliked his reputation as a notorious gunfighter. Yes, he'd taken down more badmen than most, in street fights, rural shoot-outs, and lowdown ambushes he'd survived. But that had been in his former and very legal role as a detective for Wells Fargo. He couldn't help it if the dime novelists like Ned Buntline had turned him into a damned storybook hero—a legend! Didn't people know that the definition of a legend was something that wasn't real?

Yet a pretty gal named Willa Cullen and the fine old rancher who had been her father, the late George Cullen, had managed to get him embroiled in taking down Trinidad's corrupt sheriff, Harry Gauge. And now, instead of working in the big city for the Pinks, he had allowed himself to be seduced by a pretty face and a Citizens Committee into taking over for that now-deceased crooked lawman.

As it happened, his romance with Willa had gone cold—though he sensed signs of rekindling—but that Citizens Committee had not only matched Pinkerton's offer, but thrown in some incidentals to boot. Thanks to the mayor's political connections, he was county sheriff, as well as the town's lawman, filling a marshal's role unofficially

And now the Santa Fe was about to bring a spur to Trinidad that would surely make the town boom, which made staying on as sheriff a profitable prospect.

At the table with him were four of Trinidad's most respected citizens: Dr. Albert Miller, druggist Clem Davis, mercantile store owner Newt Harris, and Mayor Jasper Hardy, the barber who kept York's beard at bay. Doc Miller, perhaps York's best friend in town, was dealing the cards, and was about to go around the table learning who wanted how many new ones.

But before that could happen, a figure who would have been unrecognizable a few months before, came hustling over to the table, saying, "Sheriff! *There* ye be!"

Skinny, bowlegged Jonathan Tulley, who had once been the town's bedraggled drunken sot, was now York's deputy. The old desert rat had sobered up, but his attire—baggy canvas pants and a dirty BVD top—had for months remained much the same, as had his reputation as town character.

Now, encouraged by the sheriff to clean himself up into a real deputy, Tulley sported clothes both storebought and clean—dark flannel shirt, red suspenders, gray woolen pants, and work boots. His thinning white hair and once-bushy beard indicated he, too, was frequenting the mayor's tonsorial parlor.

He still had the habit of waving his shotgun in one

hand, like an attacking Indian brave, but these things took time, York knew.

"What's wrong, Tulley?" York asked, his eyes still on the three aces.

The disappointment in the deputy's voice was obvious. "Why, not a dang thing! I jest been lookin' for you to report in, after my mid-evenin' patrol."

"Report then."

"Uh . . . what I said before."

"Remind me what you said before."

"Not a dang thing is goin' on. It's quiet as Boot Hill out there. Quieter!"

"Good. You say you've been looking for me?"

"I have!"

"And where am I always on Friday night?"

". . . Playin' poker with your friends, like."

"Yes. Now go have a sarsaparilla. Tell Hub to put it on my bill."

York didn't have to turn to see his deputy smile—it was in the man's voice. "Thank ye, Sheriff!"

This same scene had been enacted, more or less in the same fashion, the last five or six Fridays.

The difference was the sound of Tulley clomping over to the bar did not follow the exchange.

Now York did glance from the aces to his ace deputy. "Something else?"

"Mind if I go with coffee, Sheriff? Mite nippy out there."

York interrupted his concentration to grin. "Sure. Have cream and sugar, too, if you like."

"Thank ye, Sheriff!"

Now the deputy clomped.

"Sorry, gents," York said to his fellow cardplayers.

But the mayor, sitting across from him, was looking past York. Hardy, a slight fellow, had slicked-back, pomaded black hair and a matching handlebar mustache that overpowered his narrow face. He pointed past York, who turned to look.

Rita Filley, the proprietress, was seated at a table halfway between here and the bar. She was motioning for York's attention.

His sigh started at the toes of his well-tooled boots.

"Play without me, boys," he said, and tossed in his three aces with a growl.

Raven-haired Rita gestured for him to sit; she looked typically lovely in a dark blue satin gown, her full breasts spilling some, the rest of her almost too slender for them. Almost. She had a beer waiting for him—she was having coffee. The resemblance between her and Tulley ended there.

The heart-shaped face with the big brown eyes, gently upturned nose, and lush, red-rouged lips wore a pleasant, lightly smiling expression. But he could see through it.

"What's wrong?" he asked, pulling out a chair and sitting.

"You really don't know?"

"Rita, I'm in the middle of a game. I just walked away from three aces."

"I would think the sheriff would be more attuned to trouble."

"I'm not sheriff at the moment. What trouble?"

She nodded toward the dance floor at the end of the big room. A sort of aisle between the chuck-a-luck and roulette stations gave them a look directly that way. The honky-tonk piano was barely audible over the sound of well-oiled cowhands and the bark of the dealers and croupiers. But York could make it out: a lively version of "Clementine."

He could also see what the trouble was. Molly, a pretty little blonde in green-and-white satin, was being pawed and generally manhandled by a tall character who was weaving in a way that had nothing to do with dancing and everything to do with John Barleycorn.

"She's one of the newer ones," Rita said.

"I know. She was never a part of the upstairs festivities."

"Never. She's a nice girl. Good girl, considering."

"Considering?"

"Considering she works here. I think you can see why this isn't a job for Hub."

Hub Wainwright was a bartender but also Rita's chief bouncer—a very tough man.

But the too-friendly dance partner was a breed apart, a breed York recognized all too well. The man wore a tan silk shirt and darker brown trousers tucked in his boots— they looked new. His hair was black and curly and better-barbered than either the sheriff or his deputy. This was not somebody who did ranch work. The low-slung, tied-down Colt Single Action Army .45 in a hand-tooled, silver-buckled holster was almost certainly how he made his living.

"Signal her," York said. "At the end of the song, she sits down. If he gets rough, let me know—I'll step in."

York rose, ready to get back to his cards.

Rita touched his hand as it was pushing the chair back in place. There had been something between them once. Or twice.

Her eyes begged him. "Look at Ben Lucas—young hand from the Bar-O?"

That was Willa Cullen's spread.

"I don't see him," York said.

Her head bobbed toward the right. "He's against the wall."

York casually moved out to where he could see that Lucas was halfway out of his chair, his expression tortured, his hand already closer to his holstered weapon than might be deemed wise.

Rita was at York's side suddenly, holding onto his arm. "Ben is sweet on that child. Something might happen. Something terrible might happen."

"Ben is no gunfighter."

"But we both know that man in brown silk is."

York drew in a deep breath, let it out, nodded.

He reached in his breast pocket and got out the badge. Pinned it on the pocket. "See what I can do."

She gave him a smile that said she could just kiss him for this. Not that he'd have minded.

But he—hell, even Rita—had taken too much time talking it over. Because Ben was clambering out of his chair, just as the man in the brown silk shirt was grabbing the girl's behind in two hands.

"*You mangy son of a bitch!*"

Ben was almost on top of them when the man in brown shoved Molly aside, pulled his gun, and fired. The thunder of it was soon eclipsed by the girl's scream and then a rumble of voices around the room seemed like the threat of the storm the thunder had promised.

"*Doc!*" York called, but the heavy-set, white-haired little physician was already on his way.

Then York was standing four feet or so away from the shooter, whose gun was still in hand, smoke curling lazily from the barrel, the smell of it scorching the air.

"You just hold it right there, Sheriff," the gunny said, that .45 steady and trained right on York's chest—he'd had way too much to drink, yes, but killing a kid over a dance-hall girl can sober a man up fast.

His face was narrow and pockmarked, the eyebrows heavy and black, the eyes a light blue and his features otherwise regular, near handsome. He may have been used to having his way with girls like Molly. Not that it cut any slack with York, whose hand rested on the butt of his .44 in his own low-riding holster, though unlike the gunman's, it wasn't tied down.

Doc was crouched over Ben Lucas, a red splotch soaking a red-and-black plaid shirtfront, head hanging loose. He was a tow-headed boy who would never be a man. Or so Doc indicated, with a shake of the head.

York's nod told Doc to move away, which he did.

A queasy smile and obsequious manner came over the shooter, though he kept that gun aimed right at York. "Now this was self-defense, Sheriff. Surely that's plain. You need to know I'm a respectable businessman."

"What business would that be?"

"Why, I'm a wholesale drummer—take my catalogues store to store. Name's Burrell Crawley. This is just an unfortunate misunderstanding."

The only item this character sold was a .45 caliber.

York said, "Damn unfortunate for this youngster."

The respectable façade dropped and a snarling desperation came out. "He rushed me and went for his gun! Everybody here saw it! Just ask that little girl I was dancin' with."

"Molly?" York asked, not looking away from Crawley, whose gun was still trained on him. "Is that right? Speak up, girl."

"I . . . I . . . guess so . . ."

The supposed salesman almost yelled as he said, "Anybody else here see it different?"

If anyone had, they were keeping it to themselves.

"The circuit judge will be through here next week," York said, hand still on the butt of his holstered gun, finger slipping onto the trigger. "May be that a witness or two will testify in your defense. Maybe others will have their own story to tell. Until then, you'll be my guest."

Crawley smiled, the slight mustache emphasizing it. "Not damn likely," he said.

"You know who I am?"

"I do. You're Caleb York. And I'll warrant you're faster than me. But my gun is already out."

With a tilt of his holstered gun, York fired, blowing a hole in the toe of the gunny's boot. The wounded man howled and did another dance, even more awkward than before, as York slapped the .45 from his hand.

Between moans and whimpers and yelps, the gunny cursed York with obscenities, the like and variety of which were rarely heard even in a saloon.

York slapped him. "You're in mixed company."

Crawley lost his balance and fell hard, rattling the dance floor, winding up beside the man he'd shot, getting soaked some in the blood he'd spilled.

"Bastard!" he swore up at York.

York kicked him in the side and said, "Some of you boys sit him in a chair."

A couple of cowhands did that while York collected the .45 he'd slapped away. At least that hadn't gone off. Doc was already over, kneeling at the gunfighter's feet, lifting the left one to remove the shot-up boot and reveal a blood-soaked stocking and a mess of gore where a couple of toes should be.

York checked on Molly, who Rita was already comforting at a table well away from the dance floor. Tulley appeared at his side, looking eager as a puppy after a bone.

"Need me, Sheriff?"

"Questionable, your timing."

"Well, ye seemed to be runnin' the show."

"When Doc's through with that rabble, get a couple of these cowboys to help you haul him over to the jail."

Tulley nodded and scurried off to recruit some help.

York returned to the poker table and the little group resumed play, minus the doc. The sheriff had won two hands and lost one when Doc Miller came over, not to rejoin the play but to report on his new patient.

Leaning in, Miller said, "He lost two toes, but he'll live. Won't never dance worth a damn again."

"He didn't dance worth a damn before. Tulley and some fellas are going to haul him over to the jail. Finish anything up that needs it over there, would you?"

Doc went off to do that.

"Now," York said, "maybe we can play cards."

Two hours and a few minutes later, York—having won almost one hundred dollars from the city fathers—stopped by the jail to see how Tulley and the prisoner were doing. Since Doc Miller had returned to the game half an hour before, York already had a pretty good idea the prisoner was well in hand.

Tulley was at his little scarred-up table with a wall of wanted posters behind him, wood crackling in the pot-belly stove nearby. He was having some of his own coffee now, which was a comedown from the Victory.

"Our guest sleeping?" York asked.

Tulley shook his head. "Jest listen fer yerself—he's a moanin' and a groanin'. But I don't think he's feelin' much pain."

"Then why is he moaning and groaning?"

Tulley grinned; it was a yellow thing but had more teeth in it than you might expect. "Go on back 'n' see. But he's a mite discombobulated on laudanum that the doc done give him."

York shrugged and headed back into the little cell block.

Crawley was on his back on the chain-slung cot against the cell's rear wall. His britches were off, and his long johns were tugged up around his left ankle, the toe area of his left foot bandaged, red coming through. Seeing York through the bars, Crawley sat up.

"*Sheriff!* Sheriff, we have to . . . have to work this thing out!"

"We will work it out just fine. Like I said, the circuit court judge will—"

Crawley actually got himself off the cot and hopped and hobbled over, cringing when he put any weight on the left foot, but then he was holding onto the bars right in front of York, his face contorted. He looked like a kid about to cry.

"I *got* to be on the morning stage! People are *countin'* on me. Already bought my ticket this afternoon! You check my things that chumpy deputy of yours took offa me and see if I didn't. What I got to do is damn important!"

"You killed a man, Mr. Crawley. *That's* damn important."

He was shaking his head, face contorted with worry. "You don't understand, York. I got someplace to *be*, and it sure as hell ain't Trinidad."

"That kid you killed isn't going anywhere, and neither are you."

The prisoner pressed his face between the bars and whispered, "Look, man. I told that Wiggins feller at the livery stable he can have my horse for two hundred dollars."

"That's a lot of horse flesh."

"We're talking about a cavalry-type horse, Sheriff, fifteen hands, a thousand pounds, five years old, well-broken. You can have it yourself, or take the dollars!"

"Does sound like the horse is worth that much."

"It is! It is!"

"That boy's life was worth more."

And the sheriff left the killer there to rattle the bars until all that was left for him to do was to hobble back to his bunk.

But Caleb York couldn't help but wonder . . .

. . . *what was so important about taking the morning stage?*

CHAPTER TWO

That Caleb York had come to see the stage off pleased Willa Cullen no end.

The twenty-three-year-old young woman sported a brand-new, catalogue-ordered, dark-blue dress with a gathered waist and white lace trim at the neckline and elbow-length sleeves—with a matching jacket to take the edge off a chilly February morning.

Yellow hair braided up in back, she was a tallish Viking of a girl with an hourglass figure, who—despite delicately pretty features and long-lashed, cornflower-blue eyes—looked just about perfect for childbearing or helping with crops. But she was not married and her ranch—and it *was* her ranch now, since her father's death a month ago—was strictly cattle. That spread, the Bar-O, was the biggest in the surrounding area.

She had watched as heavy-set, bristle-bearded Gus Gullett, the shotgun guard, had loaded her luggage up into the boot at the rear of the stage. Then when she turned back toward the hotel, where out front the stage was waiting for its passengers, she'd drawn in an unbidden breath upon seeing the sheriff on the boardwalk above. Though it was only a handful of steps up from the street, he fairly loomed.

She felt irritated at herself for that giddy girlish reaction.

Yet could any woman blame her? Caleb York stood tall, broad-shouldered but lean, his jaw near jutting, his temples touched with gray but his hair, including that close-trimmed beard he'd taken to wearing of late, was otherwise a rich reddish brown. His face was a contradictory thing, sharp bones home to pleasant, even easygoing features, his eyes as light blue as denim that had seen too many washdays.

Caleb's general appearance was contradictory as well. That low-slung revolver, tied down on his thigh, said gunfighter; but his black attire—hat and coat and cotton pants and boots—said professional man. Going on a year ago, when Caleb York rode into town a nameless stranger, many had taken him for a dude. Men beaten senseless and others who fell dead under his gunfire learned otherwise.

Events had stranded Caleb, who'd been on his way to San Diego and a job with Pinkerton's, and during his unintended stay, Willa and Caleb had become something of a . . . couple. She'd been well aware he had taken on the sheriff's job "only temporary"—the position had been vacated when its previous corrupt occupant had become one of those men who fell under Caleb's gunfire. Yet the rancher's daughter felt they'd grown close enough for him to change his mind and stay around.

Before long, though, she and Caleb broke apart like cheap china when he insisted he was heading for that San Diego job after his fill-in sheriffing was done.

Only now Caleb appeared to be settling into that post, the Trinidad city fathers having lavished him with money and perquisites enough to convince him to stay on. But Willa and this man she still loved—though she would not admit that to anyone, herself included—had no real reason not to fit the broken pieces of their relationship back together.

Other than her pride.

And maybe his.

Her immediate thought upon seeing him this morning was that he had come to see her off. She was only going to nearby Las Vegas, New Mexico, to catch the train to Denver; it wasn't like she was leaving for good—a few weeks at the most. But him saying good-bye would mean something.

Then from out of the hotel, carrying a carpetbag, emerged Raymond L. Parker. The tall, white-haired, white-mustached businessman, about fifty, looked typically distinguished in his double-breasted, gray-trimmed-black Newmarket coat, lighter gray waistcoat, and darker gray trousers. That's what he'd worn to Willa's father's funeral, she recalled, though with a white top hat and not today's western touch of an uncreased, broad-brimmed gray Stetson.

Raymond Parker had been partner to George Cullen, her late father, in establishing the Bar-O. But Parker had cashed out after a time, looking for big-city challenges that he'd handily met. Mr. Parker had established businesses all across the Southwest—Kansas City, Omaha, Denver—owning restaurants, hotels, and even several banks, including the one here in Trinidad, where lately he'd been spending a good deal of time, during which he and Caleb had become good friends.

And *that* seemed to be who Caleb had come to see off. They were smiling and chatting.

Willa heard the approach of heavy footsteps and turned to witness a slender yet full-bosomed woman of perhaps twenty-five making her way toward the stage. Those heavy footfalls were not this young woman's, of course— they belonged to Deputy Tulley, who was making his bandy-legged way along sand-covered Main Street, hauling two carpetbags.

He was following after the lovely, dark-haired Rita Filley, proprietress of the Victory Saloon. She was attired in what struck Willa as just about what a saloon-owning female *would* consider appropriate travel wear—a yellow-gold dress with a floral brocade bodice, puffed sleeves, fitted waist, crinkled satin underskirt, ruffled overskirt, with touches of black fringe, silk flowers, and feathers.

Willa didn't know whether to be horrified, amused, or pitying. But *annoyed* said it best, Willa knowing this creature would be accompanying her on the Las Vegas run. In Miss Cullen's defense, it must be said that she was not generally a snob. But Willa had heard the rumors that Caleb York occasionally called on Miss Filley in her upstairs suite of rooms.

In her more generous moments, Willa might admit that she was pleased the new owner of the Victory (Rita Filley had inherited it from her late sister, Lola, about whom similar rumors concerning Caleb York's upstairs visits were bandied in town) had shut down the brothel aspect of the saloon. Now the girls who worked there were strictly available for dances and main-floor company, for the cost of a drink or two. What had been the tiny bordello bedrooms had been opened up into lavish living quarters for the mistress (so to speak) on the place's half an upper floor.

Hearing spurs and footsteps coming down the stairs

from the boardwalk, Willa turned and was pleased to see Caleb approaching. She showed no reaction, not wanting to appear forward. He tipped his hat—or rather touched his hat brim—and moved past her to help his deputy with the saloon owner's bags.

Feeling a red flush come to her cheeks, Willa turned away, not wanting Caleb to see her response. She heard Caleb and Rita talking, though not making any of it out, and then Caleb was just behind Willa, passing the Filley woman's bags up to Gus, the plump guard's face showing strain under his floppy, shapeless hat.

"Pleasant journey, Miss Filley," Caleb said, and Willa heard him opening the door for her. He was probably helping her up and in, too, but Willa didn't turn to give him the satisfaction of her noticing.

Parker was coming down those hotel stairs. He gave Willa a big smile, tipped his hat—*really* tipped it—and said, "Well, what a pleasure it will be, traveling with two such lovely ladies."

Willa managed a smile as he slipped past her, to hand up his own bag to Gus. Then she realized Caleb was standing beside her. He had a funny little smile going. What the dickens did he have to smile about?

He touched his hat brim again, nodding.

"Ma'am," he said to her.

Then he joined Tulley, and they headed to the sheriff's office.

Ma'am!

What kind of insulting nonsense was that?

Parker was waiting for her. His interest in her was strictly fatherly, and with her real father gone, that was comforting. He helped her up into the stage next to Rita Filley. Then he got up and in himself, sitting in the middle of the bench-like, leather-covered seat opposite. He took off his hat and set it next to him.

"We'll ride in comfort today," he said.

"These Concord coaches," the Filley woman said, "are much smoother than the Overlands."

"They are," Parker agreed, "but I was referring to the roominess this ride will provide. Even this smaller coach can accommodate six passengers, and there will be only four of us, I understand."

A gravelly voice from the window on the hotel side said, "Only three."

It was Norval Bratcher talking, the stagecoach driver. Parker looked out at the whip, who was checking his pocket watch.

Bratcher was a man of average height and build in a gray flat-brim hat that had once been white, and a gray handlebar mustache that had once been brown. He wore an ancient leather jacket over a dingy red-and-black-plaid shirt; his denims were faded into no color at all.

"Just the three of us?" Parker asked the driver.

"Jest you three. Fourth ticket belongs to that feller that the sheriff shot the toes off of last night. Him and his six or seven toes remainin' are languishin' in a cell at the jail. So stretch out and relax, folks. You're the whole she-bang."

Bratcher smiled brownly and spit tobacco.

This crudity barely registered on Willa, who had been around cowboys and their ilk as far back as her memory went. And Rita Filley likely knew even more about men and their disgusting ways.

Willa did not recall ever having spoken to the Filley woman, though she'd seen her on occasion. The woman and some of her girls had even come to Willa's papa's funeral, which she thought was a respectful thing for them to do, if something of an embarrassment. So when Rita turned to her and nodded, well, Willa nodded right back. It was the Christian thing.

"Miss Filley," Parker said, his smile big but not so big as to seem flirtatious, "where is it you're off to? Las Vegas itself or points north?"

"Denver," she said. Her voice was femininely high-pitched with something of an affected purr, at least to Willa's ears. "A shopping expedition. I need to pick up some things for myself, and my girls."

"Denver is where *we* are headed, as well," Parker said, with a nod toward Willa.

The big brown eyes in the somewhat dark-complected oval face got even bigger, as they swung toward Willa. "Oh, are you and Miss Cullen traveling together?"

"Not exactly," Parker said quickly, apparently realizing he might have given the wrong impression. "The branch line that will be going in this spring, connecting Trinidad and Las Vegas . . . ? I'm sure you're aware that Miss Cullen is negotiating with the Sante Fe Railroad to provide the necessary passage through the Bar-O for that spur."

"Yes," the Filley woman said, nodding. Her eyes again sought Willa. "Your father was against it, I understand. He was a lovely man, they say, one of the founders of the town. But you seem forward-looking enough to see the future can't be avoided."

Willa smiled a little. "Mr. Parker is funding the train station that will be built in Trinidad."

"On land that your father left to Caleb York."

Willa swallowed. "That's right."

"The station will be named after your father, I hear."

"That's correct."

The saloon woman's head tilted and she frowned just a touch. "I wonder if he would appreciate that, as strongly opposed as he was to the railroad coming in."

Parker, perhaps sensing an undercurrent of tension between the women, said, "I think George would in time have come around. I believe Willa would have made him see the sense of it. And I would have been at her side, helping convince him."

The Filley woman smiled and said, "I'm sure you're right. Of course, we'll never know."

Willa thought that deserved a sharp reply, but before she could summon one, Bratcher's "*Yahhh! Yahhh!*" came from above, announcing their departure, mingled with the jangle of reins and the building clop of the horses' hooves, the wooden wheels turning and cut by the occasional whinny. Citizens on the boardwalk, especially children, waved and hollered. A stagecoach leaving town, even after all these years, was still something to see—including a smaller coach like this one, with just four horses.

The Filley woman again addressed Parker. "Are you a lawyer as well as a businessman, sir?"

"Why, no. Why would you think that?"

She shrugged. "Sounds like you're representing Miss Cullen in the Santa Fe matter."

They were outside town now, stirring dust on the narrow road through nothing much. The stagecoach's continuous motion had them swaying already, with hanging leather straps to provide support if need be.

"I'm providing her with an attorney," Parker said, just a bit stiffly, "with whom I regularly do business. And as her father's onetime partner, I'm here to advise and help in any way I can. It's a privilege of age."

The saloon woman smiled. "You don't look particularly aged to me, Mr. Parker. Are you a married man?"

The question surprised him. "I was. I'm a widower."

"I'm sorry for your loss. Is it a recent one?"

"No. Over ten years past."

"And you've never re-married?"

"I never found the right . . . one."

"Well, you know what they say."

Willa asked, "What do they say, Miss Filley?"

Her smile was pursed, as if she were about to blow a kiss. "It's never too late."

The road out of Trinidad was rutted and narrow through a flat expanse broken at left by the burnt-red buttes along the horizon, their scarred black cliffs the work of rain and wind. Off to the right were the hills that grew into the Sangre de Cristo Mountains and their canyons, one of which fed the Purgatory River, so vital to Trinidad.

An awkward silence had followed the Filley woman's last remark, and finally Parker broke it, saying, "We're riding into history, you know."

Both women looked at him curiously.

He said, "Rides like this will be confined to memory, before long. When the railroad comes in, there'll be no need for a stage line between Las Vegas and Trinidad. Little or no need in the Southwest for any stages at all. Change is of course inevitable, but I feel somewhat sad about it."

Willa asked, "Why is that, Mr. Parker?"

"Please call me Raymond. Both of you ladies. The West is changing. Trinidad is changing. They have telephones in Tombstone, you know."

The Filley woman nodded. "I've heard that."

"Don't take me wrong, Miss Cullen, Miss Filley."

Neither took the opportunity to suggest he use their first names.

"I approve of change," he said. "I seek it out. But not without an awareness that something has been lost. That as we become more civilized, with a new century ahead, a way of life will soon fade from view."

The Filley woman, frowning in thought, asked, "Is that a bad thing?"

"Not bad or good. Just reality."

The coach began to come to a jerky stop. The three passengers, surprised and somewhat alarmed, were jostled fairly hard by it.

Parker leaned out his window, then said to the women, "There's a young man in the road, waving us down. Appears to be in trouble. . . ."

Willa leaned out her window. Just up ahead, off to the right, was Boot Hill, the name reflecting tradition and not landscape, as it was as flat as the rest of the dusty ground. The difference was a massive mesquite tree that made for shade and provided color enough to make a suitable home for the nest of wooden crosses and the occasional tombstone.

Right now the cemetery was fairly obscured by the dust the stopping stage had stirred.

Up top, Norval Bratcher was calling out, "*Ye need a ride, son?*"

"Be obliged," the young man said. "Iffen you can't take me back to Trinidad, might be I could tag along to the Brentwood crossroads."

Willa, leaning out, could see the slender male form in his ready-made gray shirt with arm garters and tight-waisted, loose-legged California pants of buckskin-color wool. He was clean-shaven and generally clean-looking with a big smile and friendly eyes, his blond hair short. He wore no gun belt as he moved easily, steadily toward the stage.

"Son," Bratcher's voice came, "we can't rightly head back."

The Filley woman said to Parker, "It's only half a mile. Surely we can—"

"Don't mean to trouble you none," the young man said, very near the coach now. He gestured back behind him. "My horse busted a leg and I had to put her out of her misery. Maybe they'll sell me a new ride at the relay station."

"Worth a try," Bratcher said. "Gus, help him up."

Parker leaned out and said, "The boy can ride with us."

"Sorry, Mr. Parker," Bratcher called down. "Company policy. He comes up top."

The stage swayed a bit as the new passenger was hauled up onto the seat. As that was happening, a trio of horsemen rode out from behind Boot Hill's mesquite and closed the short distance between the cemetery and the stopped coach, raising a small dust cloud. In seconds, they were three abreast, stretched out in front of the Concord, raising guns that were already drawn.

"The Hargrave bunch," Parker whispered harshly.

Willa had heard of them. Everyone in this part of the West had—led by the notorious Blaine Hargrave, they had robbed trains, banks, and, yes, stages.

"I saw him play Hamlet," Willa breathed, her heart beating fast.

Hargrave was an actor who'd come west from New York, traveling with his own company in the manner of Edwin Booth and Lotta Crabtree. But after he murdered a heckler in Virginia City, leaving without a curtain call, the next show he put on was a stagecoach robbery.

Was this an encore?

She looked out at the three men, recognizing Hargrave, all in black like Caleb—coat, vest, pants, boots, only his black hat was a flat-crown plantation number, and his shirt was white and ruffled, open at the neck to reveal a nest of hairy black, his well-carved, handsome face sporting a black mustache suiting his current role as villain, not hero.

Hargrave was center stage, of course. On his either side were the spear carriers—well, revolver carriers in this instance: a blue-army-shirt-clad man of thirty-some who resembled the boy who'd flagged them down (an older brother?) and a burly, bearded character in a plaid jacket who might have been a miner, though one who'd traded in his pickax for a revolver.

Parker drew back in, away from the window. He reached under his suitcoat and from somewhere withdrew a small pearl-handled, silver-hued revolver.

The Filley woman whispered, "You really think that little bordello gun will do the trick?"

Parker's voice was harsh but soft. "I have five shots and there's only four of them, assuming that boy is their Judas goat. Stay here and stay down."

Parker bolted from the coach and started firing.

Willa heard but could not see what happened, which was Parker's gunshot hitting the miner, who fell from his horse, while the boy's apparent brother was aiming at Parker only to have Hargrave push his arm down and spit, "Would you slay our fortune?"

On saying this, Hargrave spurred his horse and charged Parker, who fired several more times but hit nothing or no one, busy backing up, a man on horseback bearing down on him; it knocked him over, the gun flying.

This of course Willa could not see; she could only sense the stage-managed chaos all around her. She, like Rita Filley, was crouched on the floor—neither one cowering, just following Parker's directions.

Nor could she see the action atop the stage, with old Gus Gullett shoving that treacherous boy from his perch, prompting both Gus and Bratcher to grab up their shotguns. But before they could fire, Hargrave put a bullet in the stage driver's brains, a share of which departed Bratcher's head and filled the crown of his hat, which tumbled off his head and lay atop some luggage like a terrible bowl of soup.

At the same time, the boy, down on the rutted road now, pulled a revolver from under his shirt behind him and drilled three bullets into old Gus Gullett, two in his torso and one that traveled through his open mouth, shattering teeth the old boy couldn't spare on its way up and in and through his brain. Willa heard all that and later saw the results, and also heard the rattle-inducing rearing and the whinnying whining of the horses reacting to the shots.

The boy was settling the horses.

"Well done, lad," Hargrave said. He pulled his black steed to a quick stop, then stepped down as easily as a man who'd reached the bottom of a stairway.

This Willa did see, because with the shooting apparently over, she had no desire to add confusion and ignorance to her already sorry state, and was again at the window.

Parker, on the ground, appeared unconscious, his hair, his clothes, askew, his limbs as well. Hargrave, a graceful, elegant scoundrel, knelt over the businessman and looked him over.

"He sleeps, perchance to dream. . . . Reese, see how friend Bemis is doing. He's not yet among the dead, but if he doesn't stop that caterwauling, I might make him so."

The miner indeed was whimpering and occasionally yelling in pain, somewhere out of Willa's sight.

The outlaw actor, still bent over the businessman, searched his victim. He checked the man's pockets, examined a wallet, removed the folding cash from it, and tucked it away somewhere. Then he removed a gold watch from a chain on Parker's vest. He opened the timepiece. Willa could see from her window that the inside lid of the watch was engraved.

"This will do nicely," Hargrave said.

The outlaw actor got to his feet and whistled loudly— it was a shrill thing that cut the morning like a knife through soft butter. Then he called out, in his deeply resonant voice: "*Ned!*"

From Boot Hill, behind the mesquite, came another individual on horseback, leading a horse. He was in no hurry, just clip-clopping toward them. The new rider stopped his horse beside Hargrave, who handed the pocket watch up to his cohort.

"That will be all you need, friend Clutter," Hargrave said.

"Should do the trick all right," Ned Clutter said, a small, unremarkable-looking man in a homemade dark flannel shirt and duck trousers and a derby. He studied the watch with its open lid, which he then snapped shut, and pocketed the piece.

Clutter looked around, seeing what Willa couldn't from her vantage point. "Got right ugly, didn't it?"

"Are you surprised?" Hargrave asked. "Did you imagine that was fireworks you heard?"

"No. I just didn't think there'd be any killing."

"It's that no-good blackguard Crawley's fault. He wasn't on the coach."

"Why?"

"Not a clue. Had he been, he would have handled those passengers, including the illustrious Mr. Parker, who as it transpired was carrying a hideaway gun. One of those little spur-trigger affairs, probably just a twenty-two."

"Seems like it put a hole enough in Bemis to get his attention."

The miner was still whimpering, interspersed with the occasional holler.

"If he doesn't quiet down," Hargrave said, "I'll get his attention all right. Now, get going. As the natives say, skedaddle!"

"Yes, sir, Mr. Hargrave."

And the rider rode off, leaving the second horse behind, which the boy they'd "rescued" was climbing up on.

Meanwhile Parker was coming around, moaning, moving his head slowly. Hargrave got the dazed man to his feet, then walked him the few paces back to the coach and opened the door.

"Woman," Hargrave addressed Willa. "Help him. He took rather a bad fall."

Willa guided Parker back inside the coach and settled him where he'd been seated before.

"Thank you, child," Hargrave said, closing the door, with a smile as handsome as the face it was set in— devilish handsome, damn him.

"I saw you," Willa said from her window.

He seemed amused as he looked up at her, leaning a forearm against the coach. "What did you see, child?"

"Your Hamlet—in Denver. Three years ago, I think."

"Did you like my performance?"

"Then or today?" she asked.

He laughed uproariously. She couldn't tell if it was real or not. If he was acting, it was too much. If he wasn't, he was crazier than that Dane he played.

The Filley woman squeezed in nearer Willa to look out the window at the highwayman.

The saloon woman snapped, "Why are you doing this? There's no Wells Fargo strongbox on this stage. There's *nothing* of value, unless you like to dress up in women's clothing!"

"Back in the Bard's day, I might have. But not now."

Willa asked, "Are the driver and his guard all right?"

"No. They were foolish, and now have breathed their last."

The two women drew back from the window.

Hargrave peeked in. "As for what we're doing, we are indeed robbing the stage. But the item of value onboard is that disheveled character seated across from you—Raymond L. Parker."

Parker, looking like an unmade bed, had said nothing since he'd been hauled back onto the stage. He was awake but still dazed.

The saloon woman demanded, "And what of us?"

"You continue breathing at my sufferance. And with my forbearance. It remains to see if you will annoy or amuse me. As Will Shakespeare says, 'The quality of mercy is not strained'—nor is my *patience*, should you strain that."

He swept off his hat and bowed to them, an arch display of theatrics that did not amuse Willa.

"Ladies," he said, tugging his hat back on.

Then he walked toward the front of the coach. "*Reese!* Get those carcasses down and dump them on the roadside. And clean that seat up, else you'll get gore all over yourself."

"Them women—they're witnesses, Blaine."

Hearing this, Rita clutched Willa's arm, and Willa grasped the hand at her sleeve.

Hargrave was saying, "You'd leave two dead females on the road, you blinking idiot, to bring out all the law in the Southwest? Now get about your business. *Randy!*"

"Yessir?"

"Tie your horses in the back and get in. Mind our guests."

The boy did that, then scrambled back into the coach and settled next to the unconscious Parker. He had a deadly revolver in his hand and a stupid grin on his face.

Then the ride got even rougher, as the stagecoach was driven off the road toward the mountains and canyons of the Sangre de Cristo, dust boiling in its wake.

CHAPTER THREE

That the local undertaker, Casper P. Perkins, an appropriately cadaverous individual in constant black, had been the one to find the bodies in the road was both fitting and ironic.

The man had been transporting the late Ben Lucas—the hand from the Cullen spread who'd been shot to death yesterday by Burrell Crawley, Caleb York's current hoosegow guest—to be installed at Trinidad Cemetery.

Lucas had no kin anyone knew of, and Willa Cullen had done the county a favor by volunteering to pay for the burial. There'd been no service, and the prompt disposal of the earthly remains of the cowboy who'd been sweet on a girl called Molly was a practical affair—undertaker Perkins (though a skilled cabinetmaker whose coffins were second to none) knew not of embalming, and even in a chilly month like this, the sooner a corpse got into the ground the better.

So Perkins and his shroud-wrapped passenger had rattled back to Trinidad in a buckboard, the dead cowhand making an unexpected return trip, the undertaker stopping at the sheriff's office to report the grim findings.

This only seemed to support York's notion that Perkins had a way of showing up instantly after any violent death.

But for the time being the two dead bodies in the rutted road were the purview of York and Dr. Albert Miller, the lawman's friend and Trinidad's unofficial coroner, who had come immediately to the scene.

Stage driver Norval Bratcher lay sprawled facedown on the side away from Boot Hill. Shotgun guard Gus Gullett was similarly a pile of dead on the side nearer the graveyard. When Doc Miller leaned over each of them, it wasn't to check for a pulse—these two could not have been more obviously deceased if they had already been residents of the cemetery.

The white-haired, paunchy physician rose, smoothing a rumpled brown suit that had been that way before he knelt over the corpses. "No rigor yet, Caleb. Blood still wet."

York, looking like a circuit preacher in his usual black apparel, came over from the roadside where he'd been examining the place where the stagecoach had left the road. "Not long ago, then."

The doc took off his wire-framed glasses and polished them on his shirt while he pondered. "Within the hour, I would say. Single gunshots to the head. From an angle slightly below where they'd have been, seated up in the stagecoach box."

"Someone on horseback?"

Miller shrugged. "A defensible assumption. That's a diagnosis you can make better than I."

York gestured toward the yellow-brown road. "Even in hard dirt like this, it doesn't take an Indian scout to read the signs—a group of at least four men on horses did this."

"Is that them, you think?"

The physician was pointing off past Boot Hill, where a distant cloud of dust could be discerned between here and where the mountains took the horizon. Above was that clear blue sky New Mexico seemed almost to own, but a coolness and slight breeze whispered rain.

"Must be," York said, as he moved toward his black-maned, dappled-gray gelding, the animal waiting patiently along the roadside. "Again, no great tracking skills needed to see where the coach was driven off the road and headed that way, with men on horseback accompanying."

Mindful of the precious cargo on that stagecoach, York was moving fast. He was stepping boot into stirrup when the doc called, "*Caleb!*"

York swung up into his saddle as the doctor approached.

Miller's expression was tight with confusion and concern. "What in tarnation is this about? Why steal a whole damn stagecoach? Why murder both driver and guard?"

"Norve and Gus likely tried to stop the holdup, and got tickets to eternity for their trouble."

Miller was shaking his head. "But there was no Wells Fargo strongbox on that stage, no payroll of any kind. Nothing of value!"

York did not answer that directly, instead saying, "I have a bad feeling *I* caused this."

"Caused it?"

"Someone sitting in my jailhouse was supposed to be *on* that stage, keeping the people in line. Knowing Raymond Parker like I do, I will lay good odds he fought back. He carries a hideaway pistol."

The doctor's gray eyes were wide behind the glasses. "Raymond *Parker* was on that stage?"

York nodded, once. "And he is certainly 'something of value.'"

Miller frowned. "A kidnapping you mean? A ransom scheme?"

"So it would appear. And two other passengers are of value, to me anyway—Willa Cullen and Rita Filley."

Miller, who did not shock easily, clearly was. He had ridden out here in his buckboard, drawn by a Missouri Fox Trotter, who also was patiently waiting on the roadside opposite Caleb's steed.

The doctor said, "I don't believe I can load those two up by myself, Caleb."

York, up on the gelding, said, "I can't take the time. Head back to town and have the undertaker do it for you. He'll be happy to. He always welcomes new customers."

Miller sighed deep and nodded as York headed out at a good clip, heading toward that distant boil of dust.

He rode hard, but not so hard as to lose the trail the stagecoach and the multiple horses of the riders had left him, staying to one side. Much as he believed it to be the case, York could not be certain the dirty cloud he was chasing belonged to the stage. It could be something else.

So his eyes followed the coach's path through the scruffy, dusty landscape, an oddly beautiful barrenness adorned with occasional low-slung sand dunes. Way up ahead, where the hills became mountains, some occasional green showed itself, pines and such.

Caleb York had killed more than his share of men. The number, which he knew but mostly kept to himself (past thirty souls now), did not bother him. He had never put a man down needlessly and had worked to avoid doing so, in damn near every case. Yet the men whose lives he'd ended all earned the honor, and as he rode through this near desert he knew already that more killing awaited him.

That whoever had done this would also die.

Perhaps not an ideal way of thinking for a lawman, and these days an outmoded one. For a long time civilization had crawled like some poor sod caught out here with a dry canteen and no road in sight. Now civilization was racing, its thirst for change unslaked.

This stagecoach someone had snatched was a little dinosaur with wheels, jostling along on its way to extinction. The iron horse was coming. It was damn near here.

Still, York didn't imagine men would ever be so civilized that crime would go away, that greed would wither, that wanting and wanted men would be history. He had never been a gunny drifting and looking for trouble. He'd been a manhunter who sought bounty for bringing in badmen, and a detective for Wells Fargo, and now, finally, if kind of accidentally, a lawman in New Mexico.

But whichever side of a badge you were on, if you were good with a gun, you were part and parcel. You became a target yourself. For every Billy the Kid, there was a Pat Garrett; for every Clanton, there was an Earp and the occasional Doc Holliday.

The men who had done this thing were killers. The ruined bodies of Bratcher and Gullett proved that. What these killers hadn't banked on was having another killer on their trail, and Caleb York had no hesitation about adding them to his list of the dead. He didn't know who they were yet. But he knew they would deserve what he had in mind.

Yet he had not yet admitted to himself that this was personal. He made himself think objectively about the people taken on that stage. He told himself the missing passengers were still alive. Had to be, because *they* were the stolen cargo.

Raymond Parker was the obvious target. He was among the most successful businessmen in the Southwest—someone powerful, who could authorize ransom money being spent. Whether Parker would do that or not remained to be seen; he was not the kind of man to be cowed, nor to give money to men who would likely kill him anyway. So the eventual outcome there was uncertain.

And then there were the women.

What a terrible twist of fate that on that stage were the two females who meant the most to him in this life (his mother being long dead).

Willa Cullen, if he would have been capable of admitting it to himself, was the girl he loved. He did not allow himself to imagine what trouble she might be facing; this would have overridden his common sense and he'd indeed have just followed that dust cloud at the fastest possible clip.

And as the dust cloud dissipated ahead, real clouds, dark ones, began rolling in, small at first, like smoke signals, then more like smoke from an unseen fire, as if a conflagration behind the mountain range was feeding the sky, billowing charcoal clusters.

If a storm was coming, he needed to outrace it, to beat it to the men making that smaller cloud below.

He could not stop his mind from wishing he had treated Willa better. That he'd have been the kind to courtly woo her and talk her into accompanying him to San Diego and that handsome Pinkerton post. But even on horseback, following a deadly trail threatened by a dark sky, he could see the foolishness of thinking that for one moment.

Willa had been her late father's only child, the daughter who wasn't a son, and for her the Bar-O was everything. She had made it plain to York that she would hand him that spread on a platter, that he could run the ranch with her and enjoy a prosperity few in the West would ever know.

But Caleb York was no glorified cowboy. He was a detective and that meant San Diego and the Pinks. And wasn't it the woman's role to do things the way her man told her to?

He damn near smiled at that. Truth was, if Willa had been that sort, she wouldn't have attracted him in the first place. And yet how she'd *schemed* to keep him in Trinidad, in his sheriff's post, and not have him leave for California as he'd promised. Only now that he was where she wanted him—staying on as sheriff, increasingly a part of the fabric of the town—they'd been driven apart by other forces.

The thing was, things had not been the same since York killed Willa's fiancé.

Yes, the man into whose arms Willa had gone when she and York went bust was now one of those on his list of the deservedly dead. Wasn't York's fault that the son of a bitch had been after her money and land and likely plotted her very death.

But it had caused a rift, nonetheless. Even a strong girl like Willa didn't like having a wedding yanked from out under her.

Those dark clouds were stampeding into one great black herd now, and lightning was dancing in them, God growling a rumbling approval. York's coat and vest did not keep out the sudden cold, including chilling thoughts.

The other woman on that stage was Rita Filley.

The notion that he loved the saloon owner, too, had

never crossed his mind, though he knew her in a way—
the biblical one—that he did not yet know Willa. Somehow, though, York and Rita seemed more friendship than
romance. She was a practical woman, Rita, and she did
not seem to be pursuing him with matrimonial intent.

Mostly she was just a woman who did not have a man,
and since of late he didn't have a woman either, they got
together and pooled their needs, time to time. Man did
not live by bread alone, even if the Victory did serve a
free lunch.

Superficially, Rita looked nothing like Willa, being
nearly as dark as the former's Mexican mother must have
been, with eyes so brown they might have been black,
with that nice flashing quality the prettier señoritas had.

Of course, Willa's nordic blue eyes could flash, too,
like that lightning up ahead. And the women's bodies
were similar. Willa was a mite taller, but God had blessed
both gals with that nice hourglass shape so many females
these days tried to produce with straps and lacing and
such, corsets they called these instruments of torture.
Neither Willa nor Rita needed such help. Both had pretty
features in heart-shaped faces, too.

For some reason, he began to ride faster. Perhaps it
was the threat of storm as daylight gave over to prema-
ture night.

Yes, men were going to die for what they'd done.
While stray thoughts about both women floated through
his mind, he rode through rough country for over an
hour, until he was under a black sky pregnant with rain,
that single thought always returning, drumming like the
gelding's hoofbeats: *men were going to die for this.*

The storm within him seemed to feed the threatened
storm above.

He threaded through slopes until the earth turned rocky, and at the bottom of a hill that was damn near a mountain, led by the tracks of his prey, York came to a sloping road where rocks had been ground to pebbles by horses over time, a road that split off into two more only slightly nar- rower roads that led in various directions of high coun- try, around the near mountain here on its either side, and another up into and disappearing among the various peaks. Beyond those were ever higher peaks, snow-capped.

Climbing off the gelding, walking the animal past a rocky outcropping, he doubted he was tracker enough to make anything out of the combination of sand, dirt, and small pebbles of these trails.

But he looked anyway.

And before he could tell a damn thing, the sky let him have it. The rain came shooting down, the thunder full- throated now, and as he settled and soothed the gelding under a rocky shelf, any trace of which trail the stage- coach might have taken was wiped out as weather be- came the accomplice of murderers.

In half an hour the sky got the storm out of its system. The only indication of the deluge was a remaining cool- ness and puddles that were sometimes almost pools.

Nothing to do now but head back to town; what he'd put the gelding through required him to take it at an even slower, steadier pace, easier on the horse but agony on York, whose mostly pleasant memories of the two women were blotted out by fears of what they were going through.

Burrell Crawley, sleeping on the chain-slung cot in his cell at the rear of the sheriff's office, got woken up sharp.

The doc had given him laudanum again and that helped him sleep, and also took the edge off his aching foot. He

LAST STAGE TO HELL JUNCTION 41

even had his brown britches back on and the matching silk shirt. His boots remained off, however, and his foot had swollen some and the whole front part was bandaged.

His cell was not adjacent to the office, rather around the corner and down, the second of four, with only the first one looking onto the office itself. But Crawley could hear just fine from his cell, next to that one.

"Sheriff," that fool Tulley was all but yelling, "I'm right *good* and dadblamed *tired* of sleepin' behind bars at night, like I'm some kinder *jailbird*!"

Caleb York's voice came loud and steady. "A jailbird is somebody who has *already* flown the coop, Deputy. That isn't you."

"You don't have to tell *me*!"

"But you're no prisoner. It's not like you're locked in at night."

"Them city fathers, they put you in a room at the hotel! And I git a *cell*? T'ain't right. T'ain't right nohow. And you make more'n *twict* what I does! And who is it has the harder job? Do you ever do night rounds? No! Ye leave that to Jonathan R. Tulley."

"You knew what the post entailed when you signed on, Mr. Tulley. I had to do some fancy talking even to get the Citizens Committee to authorize your pay."

"Well, talk to 'em *again*! You're the great Caleb York, ain't ye? Threaten to quit iffen they don't give your loyal right-hand man his fit due and proper!"

The sound of a fist slamming down on wood—the sheriff's desk out there, no doubt—made Crawley jump.

"You listen to me, Deputy Tulley. I have more on my mind than sorting through your sorry list of complaints.

I'm dealing with a missing stagecoach and its passengers."

Tulley's voice turned hopeful. "Ye need me at yore side, Sheriff? I can back you up and show them city fathers what Jonathan Tulley is made of."

"No, Deputy. You need to hold down the fort. I'll be gone a good long while, trying to track that stage. Somebody has to be in charge, and I guess you're it. If you don't make a mockery out of this office while I'm gone, maybe . . . *maybe* I'll put in a good word for you."

The hope in Tulley's voice grew shrill. "And git me that *raise*, Sheriff?"

"Hell no! Recommend that they keep you on. Half of them already'd like to see the back of you."

A scrape obviously made by a chair's feet preceded footsteps on the plank floor, followed by the slam of a door.

Silence.

Then came stomping and Tulley's grumbling: "Dang showboat. *Big* man. *Big* gunfighter! Tellin' me what to do and what not to. Sweep out this, sleep in this here cell, stay offen that bottle! Hell with him. Hell with him, anyways!"

Crawley got to his feet, wincing at pressure on his left one, but hobbling over to the bars and hanging on, leaning half his face out as much as possible.

He watched as Tulley stumbled from the office into that first cell—with a bottle in hand.

"Consarned son of a bitch," the deputy muttered.

Crawley could see Tulley next door through the connecting bars, as the skinny, bandy-legged old boy sat down hard on the cot, making its chains creak. The bottle was raised and gulps followed. Then Tulley, who was in a long-john top and suspendered trousers, wiped his white-bearded face with a BVD sleeve.

"Big man," the deputy muttered, making a face. "Big man! Someday I'll show that full-of-hisself blowhard. Someday Jonathan Tulley'll make him pay for such ill treatment."

"Hey," Crawley said.

Tulley didn't react.

"*Hey!*" No reason to whisper: York had gone out.

Tulley looked up and blinked. "You talkin' to me, saddle tramp?"

"No need for that kind of talk. I'm a bigger victim of that puffed-up sheriff than you are, Deputy."

"I doubt that. I sincere doubt that."

"Bastard shot off two of my toes, didn't he?"

Tulley pawed the air. "You'll learn to walk with the loss, 'fore you know it. Me, I got to put up with dressin' downs and shamin' and lack of respec' every damn day of my miserable life."

"Maybe you need a new start."

Tulley snorted. "Now how's that gonna happen, you toe-shy fool? This town don't see a deputy when they see Jonathan Tulley comin'. They see the town *drunk*. They see a old *desert* rat who just follers that damn Caleb York around like a dog lookin' fer scraps, sayin' yessir, nossir. Damnit all, nohow."

Crawley widened his eyes. "Then go to some *other* town, where they don't know you. Jonathan . . . all right I call you by your Christian name?"

"Shore." Tulley frowned. "Maybe next time it'll be me catchin' the nex' stage out, leavin' this ungrateful populace in the dust."

"That's exactly how you can make a new start, Jonathan.

You go find some new town to be a new man in. That's one of the best things about the West. You just move on and start in fresh, somewheres."

The old boy's brow wrinkled. "How can I do *that* on forty a month?"

That seemed like pretty good money for this old reprobate to be making, but Crawley said, "Is that all? I had no idea you was bein' so taken advantage of." Crawley pretended to think up an idea. "Listen. I know somethin' that would benefit us both."

"You do?"

"Come over here. Let's chin a bit."

Tulley seemed to think about it some, then left his cell and came around to face Crawley through the bars.

"Speak your piece," Tulley said.

"Think maybe you could make a start with a *two-hundred-dollar* stake?"

Tulley's eyes widened. "Who couldn't?"

"That character Wiggins at the livery said he'd give me two hundred for my horse. You let me go and that money is yorn."

Tulley's brow tensed in thought, making his eyes pop some. "But what'll *you* ride, iffen you sell yore horse? How can you get away from Caleb York on foot missin' toes?"

"You let me out of this cell and I'll steal some *other* horse."

Really what Crawley intended was to hightail it to the livery and take his own damn two-hundred-dollar horse for a nice long ride, making an even bigger fool out of Jonathan Tulley.

"I want it writ down," Tulley said. "I ain't no idjit. Ye can writ some, can't ye?"

LAST STAGE TO HELL JUNCTION 45

"I can read *and* write. Bring me something to scribble on."

Tulley scurried out and came back with a pencil and a piece of paper torn off an old wanted poster. Quickly Crawley wrote out a bill of sale and handed it to Tulley.

"That's a fine animal, Jonathan," Crawley said. "You might think of keeping it and just head out for parts unknown. Smart feller like you could whip up a grubstake soon enough."

Tulley blinked at him stupidly. "Do I have to choose which, right this here second?"

"No! Think it over. By all means. But let me out of here! If York is off trying to track some missing stage, that'll give me a chance to slip away and for you to get that horse. Time's a wastin', Deputy Tully. *Former* Deputy Tulley."

Tulley grinned, said, "Be back in two shakes," and soon returned with a ring of keys. He selected one and used it, opening the cell door for the prisoner, who was seated on the edge of the cot putting on his boots. The right boot went on fine, but putting on the left one, with a foot all swelled up and missing toes, was damned painful.

Still, he hobbled out, following Tulley, who was curling a finger and leading him to the side door at the end of the small cell block. That door did not require a key, and Tulley opened it and gestured graciously for the prisoner to exit.

The door closed behind him as Crawley stepped into an afternoon that had lost its coolness and gone humid. Even so, a breath of fresh air felt good after that stuffy cell, and he was just about to hustle as best he could over to the livery when a voice called to him.

Well, not exactly "called"—more casual than that was how Caleb York, leaning against the jailhouse adobe wall, said, "You wouldn't be escaping now, would you, Burrell?"

Crawley froze.

"Hate to have to shoot you down," the sheriff said. "Unless, of course, instead of escaping, you were looking to find me."

Wincing, Crawley raised his hands and slowly turned, saying, "And why would I do that, Sheriff?"

"Well, maybe you want to tell me what the hell the gang you run with wants with a stagecoach?"

Caleb York holstered his .44 and took the prisoner by the arm and hauled him back through the side door, which a grinning Tulley held open for him. Crawley, being moved along brisk by the sheriff, was yelping now and then because of his sore foot, but that stopped when York slammed the man's behind down on the cot. Tulley was watching this with a giggling grin.

"I do right, Sheriff?" the deputy asked.

"You did fine, Tulley," York said, and handed his .44 off to him. "Now go put your shirt on. You look undignified in just the BVD top. And don't forget your bottle of sarsaparilla in the next-door cell."

Tulley, chuckling maniacally, hustled off.

Crawley was sitting slumped, eyes on the floor. He knew he'd been buffaloed.

"Could have shot you, escaping," York said, looming over the prisoner, arms folded.

Crawley nodded.

"Still could," York said. "Or I could beat it out of you, what you know."

Crawley shrugged.

"I'd just as soon give you a thrashing as not," the sheriff said easily. "Two good men were shot down dead on the road to the Brentwood relay station."

Crawley's head came up, alarm coloring the light blue eyes in the narrow, pockmarked face. "Two men ... dead?"

"Two men dead, but don't worry. You can only be hanged once."

"I didn't do it! I was right here in this cell! You know that!"

"You were meant to be part of it. Are you denying the plan was for you to be on that stage, and make sure Raymond Parker didn't cause any trouble? No, Mr. Crawley, you are as guilty of those two killings as you are of gunning down that cowboy last night."

His dark eyebrows met as if they too were in desperate thought. "What if ... what if people didn't know I was part of that gang? What if when the circuit judge comes I was to plead guilty to manslaughter where that cowboy's concerned?"

"Those are a couple of interesting 'what if's.'"

The prisoner looked like he might cry. "What do you want from me, Sheriff?"

"Mr. Crawley—I want it all."

Crawley spilled his guts.

He was indeed supposed to be the inside man when the stage hijacking took place, set to pull a gun on the other passengers and keep them in check. The target was, as York had deduced, Raymond L. Parker, for whom his Denver business partners would surely pay a hefty ransom.

York sat next to Crawley on the cot. "How will the ransom demand be made?"

"One of the gang, Ned Clutter, has a fairly smooth way about him. He'll go on to Denver and deliver the demand, posin' as a party whose own wife was on the stage, and now a hostage herself. A drop'll be arranged and Clutter would bring the cash back to where the gang is waiting."

"How much?"

"Fifty thousand."

A king's ransom, York thought.

"Where?"

"Some ghost town in the hills," Crawley said, shrugging. "I'm not from these parts. That's all I know."

"There's something you *do* know."

"No, honest to God, York—that's everything!"

"It isn't. You haven't said who you're riding with."

The dark eyebrows went up. "Oh. Well . . . the Hargrave bunch. You know them?"

He knew of them. And this wasn't good news. The former actor and his followers had left a trail of bloody corpses behind them, innocent witnesses made permanently mute.

York asked, "What does this Clutter look like?"

Crawley told him. "Do we have a deal, Sheriff?"

"A deal?"

"You back me on the manslaughter charge. Forget my part in rustling that stagecoach. Okay?"

York stood. "If I get Raymond Parker back, and the two women traveling with him . . . and if I live through the effort? I'll consider it."

Crawley moaned at the unfairness of that. Or maybe it was just his mangled foot.

Caleb York wasted no more time with the worthless

gunhand. He collected his .44 from Tulley and headed out. The rain may have washed away the outlaws' tracks, but he had a lead: Ned Clutter would likely be planning to take the last train out from Las Vegas.

York might still have time to catch him there.

CHAPTER FOUR

Willa Cullen knew now that the woman seated next to her in the coach was no longer an adversary.

Rita Filley seemed to feel the same, as one sharp, wide-eyed glance between them made their new position, their mutual plight, clear. Rita's hand found Willa's and squeezed, and the two women stayed clasped for some time, like childhood friends supporting each other as they walked through a particularly scary forest.

A rumbling sky and a sudden darkness, as if sundown had come half a day early, further made fear their companion. Just as swiftly, a coldness came upon them, God or maybe Mother Nature reminding them that, even in New Mexico, winter was here.

The stolen stagecoach, driven by an outlaw with Hargrave leading the way on horseback, rumbled along its winding upward way, joggling and frequently jolting them. Across from Willa was a still unconscious Raymond Parker, slumped in the corner between wall and window; opposite the other woman was the young blond outlaw called Randy, whose apparent brother was up top, driving with the wounded man slumped next to him.

The lad's revolver was limp in his grasp, dangling between his legs, and that unnerving grin had taken on an unsettling, lascivious aspect. His eyes looked them up and down, again and again, a starving man regarding a banquet.

"I'm Randy," he said, as they bounced with the stagecoach as it rolled over rocks.

The two women exchanged glances, affirming that each already knew this boy was randy, but Rita said, almost friendly, "My name is Rita. This is Willa."

He grinned. It was a yellow thing that might have been attractive had its hue not been so sweet-corn-colored and its bearer not had such greedy, close-set eyes, light brown but with some yellow in them, too.

"Ain't no reason," he said, "why we cain't be friendly."

Neither woman said anything, though the sky expressed its opinion by way of a growl of thunder.

"Hope we get there," the boy said, " 'fore this rain comes down."

Willa, quietly, said, "Where are we headed, Randy?"

"Next stop's Hell Junction," he said.

Rita frowned, as if that meant something to her, or perhaps it was just the implication of the word "hell." Willa thought there was something familiar about the name, but couldn't place what.

"You seem like a nice young man," Willa lied to the boy. "I'm not without means. Perhaps you could help us out of this."

"Lady, I'm who got you *in* it!" He was grinning, shaking his head. "Now, I ain't gonna be mean to you or nothin', but don't go thinkin' I can help you. My big brother would give me a whuppin' and Mr. Hargrave would like as not shoot me down. No, we three got to settle for bein' friendly is all."

Willa thought she sensed something different about Parker—was their businessman friend playing possum? Perhaps waiting for the right moment . . . ?

Willa asked, "What's your brother's name, Randy?"

"Reese. We's the Randabaugh boys." He grinned embarrassedly. "Don't want you thinkin' he whups me all the time or some such. Only if I needs it. Nobody's better to me in the whole wide world. Hostiles killed our folks when we was young 'uns. He raised me hisself. Raised me right."

Obviously.

The Filley woman, picking up on Willa working on the boy, said, "If you ever decide to get out of the outlaw life, I could use a strapping young man like you at my saloon."

His eyes and grin went wide. "You work at a saloon? You prettier than most saloon gals."

"I *own* a saloon. I bet you'd make a fine bartender. I'm always on the lookout for smart young men who can handle themselves."

His grin had "aw shucks" in it. "Might kind of you to offer, but I kinder like ridin' with Reese, and this job is gonna pay *real* high, wide, and—"

Parker lurched for the boy, grabbing at the gun that had seemed so loose in that dangling hand, only now the hand became a fist and the gun's snout got jabbed in the businessman's belly.

Hard.

With the back of his free hand, Randy slapped Parker, like a child who sassed.

Then he shoved the dignified man—who was a rumpled mess now, a trickle of red trailing down his cheek—back to his corner.

Rita said, "I was right about you." She was smiling at the boy. "You *can* handle yourself."

The boy grinned. "That I can, ma'am. That I can."

Willa admired the Filley woman for that, the remark distracting the boy and calming him down.

A few moments later the sky let loose and the rain came so hard you could barely hear the hoofbeats. Parker just sat there, no longer slumped, but glazed and dejected, his eyes now meeting those of the women, as if he were ashamed of his failure.

Perhaps he was.

Parker came out of it only enough to shutter his window, as did the women and their escort.

The hammering rain did not last long—perhaps twenty minutes—but when the shutters opened, the air stayed humid, as if the sky wanted to be able to change its mind at a second's notice. The coach was on a downward slope now, heading into a little valley between rocky hillsides.

Willa watched out her window and saw something she'd long known about but never seen: one of the many ghost towns scattered around New Mexico territory, mining camps turned bustling hamlets whose buildings were now abandoned like the dreams of getting rich quick they'd been built on. A sign at the outskirts told much of the story. The first word of HALE JUNCTION, neatly lettered, had been replaced by a free-hand jagged scrawl of red that said, HELL. A neatly lettered POP. 280 had its number crossed out half a dozen times, until the final designation (also in ragged red) was 3.

The Filley woman said, "Silver mine went bust."

Willa asked, "How do you know that?"

Her dark-eyed, dark-haired sister captive seemed to have to think before answering that. "Not much gold in these parts. . . . Anyway, people in Trinidad have mentioned it."

That answer seemed somewhat on the mysterious side, but Willa didn't follow up.

The woman said, "There's other ghost towns in these hills—coal and copper, too. If the vein isn't rich, the town dies, and everybody moves on, sometimes overnight."

Willa felt vaguely embarrassed that this relative newcomer seemed to know more about the area than she did. Of course, a woman who worked in a saloon could pick up plenty from her male clientele.

The land flattened out and the coach was soon rumbling over crushed rock down a main street where the rain showed no signs of having touched the little town. The storm seemed to have missed it, or perhaps this was not a town at all, but a mirage.

The buildings were gray and weathered, their façades paint-blistered, windows broken out or boarded up; still, it wasn't hard to imagine townsfolk like Trinidad's strolling these boardwalks, over which signs read GOOD EATS, HALE JCT LUMBER, HALE JCT LAUNDRY, ASSAY OFFICE, U.S. POST OFFICE, PALACE THEATER, BUCKHORN SALOON, LIVERY STABLE. At the far end was a dead church, its bell tower minus a bell, either scavenged or taken along to the next community. The bell was also missing from atop what had likely been a one-room schoolhouse.

The abandoned town had the expected ghostly silence, the whinnies and neighing of the slowed horses of both the coach and its accompanying riders heightened in the stillness. Wind whispered down the pebbled street, tumbleweed chasing tumbleweed. Somewhere a dog barked, sharp and high—a terrier? Somewhere else a bird cawed—a crow?

And along the low-slung boardwalk, missing planks like teeth gone from a geezer's smile, scurried small animals, squirrels on the left, rats on the right, each little army keeping to itself.

A rodent by any other name, Willa thought.

At the livery stable, down near the dearly departed church, Hargrave got down from his horse and opened the double barn doors. The coach was driven in, the driver getting down to help Hargrave unhitch and then guide the stage's horses into stalls.

The outlaw in the blue army shirt, whose blond-haired resemblance to the boy made him Reese, the brother, approached Hargrave while Willa watched out her window. Rita couldn't see much from hers but was doing her best. Parker seemed morose, staring at nothing except, perhaps, his limited prospects.

Down on the straw floor of the livery, Reese was saying to the gang leader, "Enough room to stable our hosses right here, Blaine."

Interesting, Willa thought. *Some of these outlaws called the head man "Mr. Hargrave," but this one used the actor's given name. Second in command, perhaps?*

"No," Hargrave said. "We will instruct Broken Knife to hitch our steeds outside the Inn."

The Inn? she wondered. *What in blazes was the Inn? And who or what was Broken Knife?*

Hargrave said, "We'll be safe enough there, but one never knows when . . . how does the cliché go?"

"The what?"

"One never knows in this life when one must make a fast getaway."

Shakespeare hadn't said that, Willa thought.

"Oh," Reese said. "Right."

"We'll let Mr. Bemis rest up on top of the coach till we get these women and our honored guest suitably housed."

"Should we round up a doc for Ben?"

"Our remedies oft in ourselves do lie, my friend."

Now that *was Shakespeare,* Willa thought.

"You mean, if he dies he dies?"

"I mean we will not risk taking that step unless necessary . . . *Boy!*"

Randy stuck his head out his coach window. "Yessir, Mr. Hargrave?"

"Escort our guests across the street, would you? There's a good lad."

"Yessir."

Randy waved his gun at Parker and nodded toward the coach door. Parker opened the door and stepped down from the coach, using the fold-down step unsteadily, but obeying.

Hargrave was waiting, looking like a pirate with his ruffled shirt, curling chest hair, and black jacket and pants. But it was a long-barreled revolver, not a cutlass, that he pointed at the dejected businessman.

Randy smiled—such a pleasant, almost handsome boy, if dim—and gestured with the hand that didn't have a gun in it.

"Ladies," he said. "Best watch your step."

Willa climbed down from the coach first and stood beside Parker, who didn't meet her eyes. The stable smells, manure and hay, were strong and almost comforting to a girl raised on a ranch. The horses, after the long ride, were still settling. The outlaw called Reese was wiping one animal down.

The Filley woman stepped from the coach and, judging by a momentarily startled expression that became a knowing little smile, Willa could deduce Randy must have put his hand somewhere it didn't belong. The dark-eyed woman winked at Willa, as if to say, *Our best chance to escape is right behind me.*

Willa nodded, barely, as if to say, *You are not wrong.*

Randy took Parker by the arm, sticking the snout of the gun in the man's side, and directed Willa and her companion to walk in front of them.

"Just across the street and down to the left some," the boy said.

The two women both wore button-up boots, with slight heels, which made for steady enough walking, but the crushed rock underfoot was awkwardly navigated nonetheless. Willa stumbled and the Filley woman caught her by the arm.

"Got you, Willa," she said.

Willa glanced at her. "Thank you, Miss Filley."

That came off in a way Willa hadn't intended.

"I mean to take no liberty," the other woman said. "But I think we are at the point where using each other's first names is only natural and right. Please call me Rita."

"Please call me Willa."

They smiled at each other, Willa weakly but indeed smiling.

And then there it was, with a high-riding sign by way of identification: HALE JUNCTION INN in red-edged black letters, though the HALE here had also been replaced with a jagged scarlet HELL. The front of the place was wider than most businesses along Main Street, and though its windows were boarded up, the façade had seen a white-washing within recent memory. The boardwalk out front bore no missing planks, and no vermin were in sight, except the human one escorting them. While it didn't shout its difference from the neighbors, and did not stand out, the inn was not your usual ghost-town hovel.

For half a second, Willa took the small dark figure standing near the doors with arms folded for a cigar-store Indian, but then realized this statue with its immobile carved features was a living, breathing man—red turban, blue army jacket, buckskin trousers, high leather boots, knife at his hip, and a rifle propped against the wall. He was the guard at the gate. Only those dark watchful eyes moved.

This must be Broken Knife.

The women paused under the overhang before double doors, heavy carved dark wood ones that, unlike the school and church bells, for some reason hadn't been scavenged; and the window panels were stained glass—unbroken!

"Allow me," came the cultured baritone of their captor.

They hadn't noticed Hargrave catching up with them, and Willa started a bit when he announced himself. Rita gave her a raised-eyebrow look.

"Your luggage will be brought to you," he said, with a sweeping bow.

Was that supposed to be funny, Willa wondered, *or could he really be that pompous?*

The man in black and ruffled white opened both doors

for the women, stepped aside for them to go in, then followed, shut those doors, and hovered. What the women
found within was not lavish, but neither was it something
normally found in a ghost town.

They were in a hotel lobby. Nothing else about it was
as fancy as those stained-glass doors, and the interior had
not been maintained as well as it might have been, had
the rest of the town been alive and well. But this interior
was relatively clean, and the various chairs and sofas,
scattered around where the lobby opened up into a parlor at the right, were holding onto their stuffing, and
even a couple of potted plants were apparently getting
enough water to survive.

At the left stairs rose to guest rooms, apparently, with
a check-in desk tucked back and facing them, behind
which was a plump little man with a practiced smile
waiting before his wall of keys—round-lensed spectacles
perched on his red knob of a nose, his white hair was a
wispy memory, his full cheeks home to the white bristle
of an indifferent, infrequent shave, and his black vest and
high-collared white shirt had a slightly dingy look.

The whole place did. The carpeting was faded and
frayed, but it was carpeting, all right, with a fancy black-
and-white pattern. The parlor's stone fireplace way off to
the right had Indian pottery along the mantle; antlers
rode the surrounding wall. Something about the Inn reminded her of an off-season resort before a maintenance
and cleanup crew had arrived.

Into this area, Randy guided Parker to an overstuffed
leather chair, the businessman looking dejected and
dazed. The boy lingered nearby, keeping an eye trained
and his pistol in hand. Willa and Rita remained in the
outer area with Hargrave.

"Welcome, ladies," said the man behind the check-in counter.

The two women said nothing.

The desk man's voice was a raspy, high-pitched, folksy thing. "No need to be shy, ladies. Step right up, step right up."

After exchanged glances and eyebrow shrugs, they responded to this carnival-barker entreaty and walked to the counter, Hargrave looking on with obvious amusement.

"What a pleasant surprise you are!" the chubby elf of a man said. "Oh, excuse me. I should introduce myself." He lowered his head and touched his chest with short, fat fingers. "I am the proprietor of the Hale Junction Inn— Wilmer Wiley. You'll meet the Mrs. Wiley soon enough. Her name is Vera and she runs a tight ship."

Rita asked, "We're a surprise?"

"Yes, and, as I say, a pleasant one. I had not been told we would have guests of the female persuasion. But, as it happens, we can provide you lovely ladies with a room to share, as soon as our colored girl dusts and straightens up a bit." He looked past the women. "Will that be to your liking, Mr. Hargrave?"

Hargrave stepped forward, his black hat in hand; he was always ready to take center stage.

"Quite suitable," he said. "Add their rooms to my bill . . . and I will put money in thy purse for meals, as well." His attention turned to Willa and Rita. "Ladies, there is no need for you to sign the guest register. This is a special sort of hostelry."

What in heaven's name kind of place is this? Willa wondered.

Hargrave was saying, "For the sake of civility, good ladies, what appellations might you answer to?"

Willa hesitated, but her companion said, "I'm Rita. This is Willa." Last names were conspicuously absent.

He gestured with an open hand. "Lovely names for lovely ladies. We will get to know each other better when time allows. For the nonce, I must deal with my wounded comrade."

Another bow, and he made his exit.

Rita raised an eyebrow and said softly, "For the nonce?"

"At least he's a gentleman."

Very softly Rita said, "For a kidnapping murdering stagecoach bandit."

Their rotund, elfin host gestured toward the parlor. "Ladies, if you'll make yourself comfortable, perhaps I could offer a potable? Not too early for wine, you think?"

Not for him, most likely.

Willa said, "Do you have coffee?"

"My, yes," he said, eager to please. His twinkly eyes lived under bushy white brows. "And you, my dear?"

Willa said, "Tea, perhaps?"

"Tea it is."

He came out from behind the desk and waddled through the wide archway into the parlor. The women followed him, hanging back some, then paused as he cut left. Through open double doors in a wall of wood and mostly glass, the innkeeper entered a typical if modest hotel dining room where tables bore no cloths and framed landscapes hung crooked. At the back left, he slipped through a door that was presumably to the kitchen.

Rita looked at Willa with wide eyes, and Willa did the

same to Rita. Then the pair looked around at the over-stuffed furnishings and stone fireplace and looming deer heads. Parker was already seated, lost in gloom.

Randy came over to the women, equally eager to please. "Not what you expected, huh?" he asked, and laughed like a horse with something caught in its throat. "Like a fancy hotel in Denver or such like."

"Oh yes," Rita said.

Oh no, Willa thought. *Nothing like Denver.*

But exactly like a mining town hotel gone to seed. This must be what the Inn had been like during the months of Hale Junction's decline into abandonment.

Only, why was it still here? And some kind of going concern?

"Make yourself to home," the boy said, as if delighted he could show them such a good time. "I best get over to the livery and help Mr. Hargrave. You gals stay put."

He started out, then stopped, turned, the friendliness gone.

"Best you pay heed," he said firmly, gesturing with the gun in his hand, not threatening, just a thing he happened to be holding. "Ol' Wiley'll call the troops out on you, and his wife is mean as a rattler and will shoot you soon as look at you. And Broken Knife, standin' guard out there? That's just his name. His knife ain't broke at all."

Willa just looked at him. Rita managed a smile and a nod. Then he was gone.

Alone with Parker, the women stood on either side of the seated man, who stared straight ahead.

Willa asked, "Are you all right, Mr. Parker? Are you hurt?"

Quietly, he said, "I am ashamed."

Rita frowned at him. "Why ashamed?"

"I failed you both. First I risked all of our lives by clumsily attacking those outlaws, managing only to get that poor stage driver and his guard butchered. Then I made an attempt to take down that fool boy and he bested me."

"I know a little Shakespeare myself," Rita said. "What's done is done. Isn't that Shakespeare? *Hamlet* or something?"

"*Macbeth*," Willa said. She leaned in, rested a hand on his shoulder. "You have to pull yourself together, Mr. Parker. It's the three of us against these outlaws, and I don't think the people running this hotel are much better."

Parker was still gazing straight ahead. "It seems to be some kind of outlaw hideout. But we are outnumbered and that Hargrave character is no fool. I bitterly regret the position I've put you ladies in."

"Enough of that," Rita snapped. "We have to think. You're of value to them—*you're* the strongbox they took off the stage."

He nodded again. "Clearly they intend to ransom me."

Willa said to her, "But the brother of that boy called Rita and myself witnesses. He wanted Hargrave to *kill* us. Perhaps he still will."

Rita sighed. "I agree. Those rooms that two-bit Santa Claus says he has for us could be out back, getting dug while we speak. We clearly weren't part of the plan. The gunman who killed that cowboy of yours, Willa, last night at the Victory? I think he was their inside man who got derailed into a jail cell by our mutual friend, Caleb York. Those murders today weren't intended. Hargrave and his bunch meant to stop the stage, grab *you*, Mr. Parker, and ride off with the means for their ransom."

Parker huffed bitterly. "And had I not been so impulsive, that is what the outlaws would have done. And those two men would be alive, and you two would be safe."

"Stop it," Rita ordered. "That doesn't do any of us any good, you whipping yourself. We need to think. I can bargain with my body, and Miss Cullen can do the same, if she's willing. But even so, after these lowdown bastards have had their way with us, six-foot-under 'rooms' out back are likely waiting. That pretentious highwayman may *think* he's Hamlet, but he's just another Simon Legree."

Those words had barely passed Rita's lips when the front doors opened and the boy and his brother hauled in the limp, unconscious form of Bemis, the outlaw resembling a miner who'd been shot by the stagecoach driver, as his bloody shirt testified—Randy at the shoulders, walking backward, Reese carrying the man under the knees.

Hargrave had held a door open for them, and now he stepped inside as the brothers paused with their cargo. The actor yelled, "*Wiley! Attend us!*"

The master of the house emerged from the kitchen with a tray on which were two shaky cups, one of tea, one of coffee, which he managed not to spill much of, delivering them to a small table near where the two women stood, then all but sprinting to his client.

Wiley smiled obsequiously and pressed his hands together before him. "How might I be of service, Mr. Hargrave?"

"Do you have a spare room on this floor?"

"Only the quarters of Mrs. Wiley and myself."

"Is there a bedroom?"

"There are two—mine and hers. I use the guest room. My darling bride cannot abide my snoring."

"Your room will do. Direct us."

With only a pause to quench his disappointment at this inconvenience, Wiley said, "Of course, Mr. Hargrave," and led the way, which took them through a door to the left of the stairway.

Before long, from behind the closed doorway to the Wiley living quarters, came a terrible cry of pain. Apparently, getting Bemis settled on the bed had wakened the man.

A woman came streaking down from the second floor. Striking, with beautiful features that hard living had coarsened, her long dark hair curling loose at her shoulders, she took the stairs, quick and hard, as if she were angry with them. She stopped two-thirds of the way down.

"*Blaine! What the hell goes on?*"

She wore a white peasant dress with a red sash and her complexion was dark, darker than Rita's. She appeared to be full-blooded Mexican, and the low-cut dress emphasized her overwhelming voluptuousness.

Blaine appeared in the doorway to the innkeepers' quarters.

"Juanita, my *querida*," he said, "friend Bemis was wounded on the job today. He may yet breathe his last, but we're looking after him as best we can. Did we disturb your siesta?"

Something about that last bit sounded sarcastic to Willa.

Juanita came down to meet Hargrave at the foot of the stairs. Though much shorter than him, she had a certain stature; she stood with her hands on her hips, her chin up, her bosom out.

"You will get yourself killed, *querida*," she said, "if

you are not careful. This job you pull, it was very dangerous. *Muy arriesgado.*"

"Oh, what men dare do, to please their woman! To give her nice things." He made a sweeping gesture. "Have you met our guests?"

She frowned as she took in the three strangers in the parlor off the lobby. Slowly, her eyes narrowed, like a cat prowling for prey, the Mexican woman approached the well-dressed older man in the leather chair and the two nicely garbed young women standing on either side of him.

Without addressing them, she said over her shoulder to Hargrave, who had slowly followed her, "This is the banker, the businessman. But who are these *mujeres inútiles?*"

"Mr. Bemis was not the only casualty, *mi amor.* We had to dispose of two employees of the stage line, who objected to our intrusion. These young women were along for the ride. We have decided to make them our guests."

She turned, eyes flaring. "*Testigos?* And you did not leave them *sangría?* There on *la carretera?*" She shook the mane of black hair and stalked off, heading back up the stairs, muttering, "*Hombre tonto,*" her footsteps quick but heavy.

"My apologies," Hargrave said, bowing yet again, and returned to the Wiley quarters.

Willa said, "She's a danger. Could be the death of us."

"Or the life," Rita said with a smile, arms folded. "She's not an ally, but she may be useful."

Willa couldn't see how.

Parker had been watching all this with a new alertness. The women deposited themselves on a two-seater red-and-black brocade sofa nearby. Both watched the businessman with keen interest. Several glances affirmed that they shared a sense that a new attitude had worked its way through his despair.

"We'll find a way out of this," he said. "I give you my pledge."

That heartened Willa.

But she'd rather Caleb York were making that promise.

CHAPTER FIVE

Getting to the relay station at Brentwood Junction took Caleb York under twenty minutes, but he had to ride hard.

He'd been pushing the black-maned, dappled-gray gelding all day, and figured it would be best to leave the animal here. He would pay Irvin Fosler, who ran the station, for the use of a fresh horse for the journey to Las Vegas, hoping to make it there by mid-evening, before the late train to Denver pulled out.

That was how he figured Ned Clutter—that was the name Crawley had given him for the Hargrave gang's ransom messenger—would get himself to the Mile High City and Raymond Parker's business partners.

Slowing the gelding to a trot, York neared the humble array of gray, weathered buildings—barn, corral, main station—and paused at the wooden-fenced enclosure where a dozen of the compact stallions called Morgan horses were milling, mostly black, a few bay or chestnut.

At the relay station building, an unpainted shabby structure with a sagging plank porch, York dismounted and hitched his gelding at the leather-glazed post next to a saddled horse tied there. His slitted eyes regarded the animal's roan coat with suspicion.

At the jail, when York questioned Crawley, the prisoner had given him a description of Ned Clutter that had been on the vague side—small, not fat, not thin, with a thick black mustache, claiming no recollection of what the man had been wearing. But Crawley did say Clutter rode a roan.

Could this steed be the gang's ransom messenger's?

It was mid-afternoon now. If Clutter had stopped to eat and have a few beers, he might still be here. Short of knocking on a ranch house door, Brentwood Junction was one of the few opportunities for sustenance on the way to Las Vegas.

York nodded to himself, then took off his badge and tucked it away in the breast pocket of his black shirt.

When he went through the saloon-style batwing doors into the low-ceilinged space—modest bar at the left, scattering of dining tables at the right, the sort of unpainted, unprepossessing premises typical of a relay station—York tossed a polite smile at the little man seated at the counter, hovering over a plate of mostly eaten beans and stew.

This man who might have been Clutter frowned a tad, then gave a noncommittal nod to York and went back to wiping a torn tortilla through the remains of a serving of the spicy beef stew on offer here.

In back of the counter was short, lean, bandito-mustached Fosler—an Irishman with a Mexican missus—clad as usual in a bartender's black bow tie and a white shirt with apron. His smile, upon seeing York enter the shabby establishment, was a nervous one, perhaps because once upon a time the sheriff (before he wore a badge) had shot some people dead in here. Including the former sheriff, as it happened, a corrupt bastard who called for killing.

York gave Fosler a tiny, squinty head shake and quickly touched where his badge usually lived. The man who was possibly Clutter had his back to York now, and the relay station man got the message.

York ambled to the counter and sat, putting a stool between himself and the other patron, who had half of a big mug of beer left. There were only four stools.

With an easy smile, taking off his hat and putting it on the counter to his left, York said to the relay station man, "Got a ration of that tasty stew of Maria's left, Irwin? Or did my friend here get the last of it?"

Fosler's smile was pitiful. "There's always some for *you* . . . good sir."

That awkward substitute for "sheriff" didn't seem to register on the small mustached man who was reaching for his beer. His hat was off, too, a derby resting on the stool at the right; his pale yellow hair was curly. The potential ransom deliverer wore a gray shirt with black sleeve garters and light brown duck trousers. He had a Colt Single Action Army .45 holstered on his right hip, not tied down, but always a formidable weapon.

"Fix me up a plate," York said to Fosler, "and a beer."

The relay station man got busy getting that together.

York turned to his fellow customer: "That your roan out there?"

The curly-haired little man with the big gun wiped foam from his mustache and frowned. "Yeah. What is it to you?"

The man's voice was reedy, kind of high-pitched, not suited for threats.

York held up his hands, palms out, grinned. "Nothin' at all to me, friend. Just a handsome animal is all. Where you headed?"

"Is that *your* business . . . 'friend'?"

York shrugged. "Not unless you're headed to Las Vegas, too."

The little man swung around on the stool and frowned at the questioner. "What if I am?"

York offered another shrug. "Long ride like that, thought you might like some company. Headed that way myself."

"Not agin it," the little man admitted with his own shrug, talking as he chewed the last of his tortilla. "But you'll have to catch up with me. I already et and I ain't waitin' around for some stranger to do the same."

"Fair enough."

The little man pushed his empty plate forward, only a few gulps of beer remaining to maybe keep him here a while, and said, "What's *your* business in Las Vegas?"

"Well, we got that in common."

"How's that?"

York gave him just half a smile this time. "It's *my* business."

Fosler, not any more skittish than a virgin at her first dance, spilled some stew as he put down the plate of it and beans and tortillas in front of York, who began to eat the stew, using his left hand. Keeping his right hand free in certain situations was a practice a gunfighter like York had long since taken up.

"Irwin," York said, calling the proprietor over with a curled finger. "I'd be obliged if I could leave my gelding here and borrow one of your Morgans. I been riding a while and could use a fresh mount. By this time tomorrow, I can swap you back. Be an eagle in it for you."

"Sure, be glad to . . ." The "sheriff" seemed to catch right behind the bartender's teeth. ". . . sir."

York dug out the gold coin, which was worth ten dollars, and—again, using his left hand—tossed it on the counter, where it rang and settled.

Fosler grabbed up the coin in a greedy fist, then backed away with a smile that was half again too big, saying, "Excuse me, gents. My cook, Maria—I think she needs some help."

She hadn't called out for any, but neither customer questioned their skinny host. Maria was Fosler's wife or anyway his woman, and was anything but skinny.

The little man sent his eyebrows up and down, saying, "He's a jumpy one."

"Ain't he though? If you want another beer, I'll call him back out here. I could eat fast and you could drink it slow, and maybe we could ride out together. Name's Cal Wilson."

York did not offer a hand to shake.

Nor did the little man, who said, "John Smith."

York grinned. "No kiddin'. I bet they give you a hell of a time when you check in to a hotel. Of course, it would depend on the hotel."

The little man said nothing, shrugged. "I'll take that beer."

"My treat."

York called out for Fosler, who emerged from the back with narrowed eyes; he was polishing a glass that was not likely to have been washed.

"Yes, sir?"

"Give my fellow traveler here," York said, "another beer."

Fosler said, "Yes, sir."

The bartender produced another warm mug and set it on the counter, then gestured toward the rear, making a plaintive face.

"You go help Maria," York said, waving him back. "I'll holler if we need anything."

York got back to eating, using his left hand as before, and worked at putting the food and the accompanying beer away quickly. But John Smith was impatient nonetheless, and dug out a watch to check the time.

The watch was a gold one, and York recognized it—*a timepiece engraved to Raymond L. Parker by the late George Cullen.* He couldn't see that inscription from where he sat; just that frilly writing rode the lid, but the fancy timepiece was unmistakable.

And it was clearly the kind of proof that Ned Clutter might provide Raymond Parker's associates of their friend and partner indeed being in outlaw hands.

When John Smith tucked the watch away in a pocket, York drew his .44 in an eye blink and said, "You're under arrest, Mr. Smith. But my name isn't Wilson and yours isn't Smith."

An awful grin appeared under the dark mustache and dark eyes glittered. "I was *wondering* why that son of a bitch was 'sir-ing' you. You'd be Caleb York."

"I would be."

"Heard you turned lawman somewhere in these parts. Saw your picture once. Beard kind of threw me."

"Cold weather's comin' on," York said, his spurs jangling as he stepped down. The two men were only maybe three feet apart. "Now slide off that stool nice and easy, and keep your hands up, palms outward, waist high."

Clutter nodded, started to move slowly off his roost, then grabbed his plate and swung it into York's wrist, the edge of the thing landing hard, and snapping into pieces.

The impact and sharp pain that went with it was enough to open York's fingers and send the .44 tumbling from his grip. As he dove after the weapon, the man with Parker's gold watch drew down on the sheriff and shot twice, the roar of the gun rattling everything in the room not nailed down. Bullets chewed up dirty wood flooring as York rolled toward his fallen revolver. When the .44 was again in his hand, York fired toward Clutter, body shots, not head shots, not wanting to kill the man, preferring to have him alive and talking.

But that wouldn't be happening, as one of York's three bullets angled up through Clutter's throat while the other two went through him like Indian arrows, going in small but coming out bloody, splashing a wall in back of the counter that the relay man would finally have to get around to cleaning. The .45 pitched from limp fingers and clunked to a stop.

Clutter slid down the stool behind him, knocking it over flat on the filthy floor like a second victim. The little man's eyes were very big and he was gasping and making a terrible sound, like a drowning man, only it was his own blood he was drowning in, reddish froth coloring his mouth and mustache a smeary, bubbly scarlet.

"Goddamnit!" York said, getting up.

Cordite scorched the air as the sheriff walked over in the vain hope that Clutter might have survived; but when he got there and knelt to the man, he saw the dark eyes cloud over with nothingness.

Fosler and his plump wife peered out from the kitchen doorway, her head over his, totem-pole style.

"Is it over, Sheriff?" Fosler asked, his voice small after the thunder of gunfire in the small space.

"Yes," York said.

"Who . . . who *was* he?" Fosler came out, and glanced sideways with a frown at the red, gloppy splotches dripping down his already grimy wall.

"His name was Ned Clutter. He was one of the Hargrave bunch."

From the kitchen doorway, Maria said, "I hear of them. Bad men."

"Bad men," York agreed, and stood. "One less of 'em now."

Fosler was shaking his head. "Could you wait to settle up with my customers, Sheriff, till they settle up with me?"

"Not my intent." He holstered his gun. "I was just trying to stop him."

"You did that, all right. You . . . you still need that horse, Caleb York?"

"No." He was pinning his badge back on now. "The one favor this dead bastard did me was spare me a long ride to Las Vegas."

York told the relay station man that he would be going back to Trinidad and would send Doc Miller out to collect the corpse.

And York, on the gelding, headed out to do just that, knowing he'd succeeded in intercepting the ransom messenger, but not knowing how, or even if, that was any help to Raymond Parker.

Or Willa Cullen.

Or Rita Filley.

*   *   *

By late afternoon, York was back in his office behind his desk, sitting up. His feet were on the floor, his gun still strapped to his hip, though he'd untied the weapon. Wouldn't do for it to fall on the floor and discharge. That would be all he needed on this damn day.

He had already dispatched Doc Miller to make a trip to the relay station, which exasperated the physician, who had put in a long hard day himself.

"Judas priest, Caleb," Doc had said, as the sheriff helped him up onto the buckboard, "my dead patients are beginning to outnumber the living ones."

"Good ammunition," York said, with a salute of a wave, "for me making your case with the Citizens Committee. You deserve a salary and the official coroner title."

"Don't I just," Miller said, shook the reins and got his horse's attention, and man and beast rumbled out of town, both making unhappy noises.

Deputy Tulley was seated in a chair by the scarred table that was as close to a desk as he was ever likely to have. Like the faces on the wanted posters pinned up on the wall in back of him, Tulley was staring at the sheriff, the old desert rat leaning forward with an alertness that came with staying on the wagon for some months now.

The deputy said, "Does sound like ye got yourself in a fine fix, Sheriff."

"I'm a trigger-happy fool. Do I have to kill everybody who takes a potshot at me?"

"Strikes me as a pretty fair policy. But that there Hargrave bunch'll start wonderin' in a day or two why their man ain't come back with that ransom money."

"Doesn't work that way, Tulley," York said. He took a

swig of his deputy-made coffee from a tin cup; it dated to this morning, at which time it could have curled the bark off a tree. The brew had not mellowed with age.

"How *would* they have worked it?"

York raised an eyebrow. "Likely a drop would be set up. Some agreed-to place where the money could be exchanged for the prisoner. Somewhere that provided high lookout perches, so the law could be spotted if Parker's people didn't follow orders."

"A canyon, maybe."

"A canyon, yes. They're up in the hills, or even the mountains. Our prisoner told us the bunch was holed up in some ghost town. . . . How *is* our prisoner?"

"Oh, he sleeps deeper than that feller you shot today. The doc stopped by. Got him loaded to the gills with laudanum. Losin' toes is pretty miserable, I reckon."

"Losing your life is worse. Son of a bitch is lucky I didn't kill him."

"Shore is," Tulley said. "Trigger-happy fool that ye be."

York grinned and laughed, and so did Tulley.

"You lived half your life in those hills and mountains," York reminded his deputy.

"Oh, more'n half. Why?"

"You must know every ghost town in those hills and valleys and mountainsides."

"Purt' near," Tulley allowed.

"How many do you know of?"

Tulley leaned back in his chair and got to thinking. "Oh . . . offhand . . . I reckon I know of mebbe half a dozen."

"Close to Trinidad?"

"Close enough, in most cases."

"Close *together*? So that we could go from one to another and shake the trees for those bastards?"

Tulley shook his head. "No, Caleb York, I fear that
ain't practical. They is here and there and everywhere.
Got no real fix on where any of 'em is located at. I just
know they's up there, somewheres. Oh, we could do
what you say but might be at it for days. And days. Be a
real chore."

York sighed. "In the meantime, Raymond Parker and
those two women are in the hands of Hargrave and his
outlaw rabble."

"Outlaw rabble," Tulley pointed out, "does not have
respect for the gentler sex. If I was a beautiful woman, in
cruel hands like that? Why, I'd sooner slit my throat than
give up my honor to ruffians of that nature."

Tulley meant well, but the sheriff did not care to picture a female version of the reformed desert rat, particularly being compromised. And the old boy did not seem
to have any real idea where any of the ghost towns were
located.

"Tulley, hold down the fort," he said, getting to his
feet. He grabbed his jacket off the wall peg, but left his
holster tie-down loose. He'd be sitting again soon. The
sun hadn't set yet, but the game would be going by now.

"Poker, Sheriff?"

"Poker, Deputy."

"T'get yore mind off unpleasantness?"

"Actually, no. I think there's a good possibility I may
learn something."

"About poker?"

"Hardly. About something else entirely."

Climbing into his jacket as he began his walk to the

Victory several blocks down, York let the coolness of the evening soothe him, enjoying the look of the little main street at dusk. Lamps in the upstairs windows of living quarters were glowing yellow eyes in the faces of businesses, all of which were shuttered, except of course for the saloon.

Not hard to imagine Trinidad turning ghost town itself. Probably would have, if Willa Cullen hadn't gone against her late father's wishes and agreed to sell the right-of-way to the Santa Fe Railroad for their spur to Las Vegas. Willa had a mind of her own. She was a strong girl. A strong woman.

But as he approached the saloon, he thought of that other strong woman. Laughter and bustle floated from around the batwing doors of the Victory, whose lights were not so much yellow eyes in the twilight, as more a flickering fireplace a man could warm himself to.

For a weekend night, payday weekend, the festive nature of the Victory was almost subdued. Only a few satin-clad lasses trolled the cowboys and clerks for drinks, no piano going, no dancing. Maybe word had gotten around about their owner's peril. Certainly the staff knew, head bartender Hub Wainwright and the rest.

Yes, Rita was a strong woman, too.

She was also a good businesswoman. That's why she provided that special table for the city fathers to play poker without dealer Yancy Cole sitting in. Rita knew how important it was to stay on the right side of the Citizens Committee.

This was a game where York was always welcome. Tonight's players included well-groomed, diminutive Mayor Jasper Hardy, town barber; muttonchopped hardware-store man Clarence Mathers; skinny, bug-eyed apothecary

Clem Davis; and heavy-set, blond, mustached mercantile-store owner Newt Harris.

A chair was waiting for the sheriff. He was welcomed with smiles, then words of support and sympathy for the terrible doings earlier. They were between hands. They passed him the deck and York began to shuffle the cards distractedly.

The mayor said, "Have you considered raising a posse, Sheriff?"

"No."

Harris sat forward. "But the word around town is that this is the Hargrave gang. Surely you don't intend to go after such villains by yourself."

York had kept under wraps that he'd killed the ransom messenger. These people didn't need to know that. He wished he didn't have to know that himself.

"I might gather men with guns," he allowed, "if I had a plan of assault. But that downpour today made further tracking impossible. I lost them in the foothills. At the base of the foothills, truth be told."

With sympathy in his voice, Mathers asked, "Nothing to go on?"

"Oh, I have something to go on, all right. Hard to follow up on, though."

The mayor asked, "What *do* you have, Caleb?"

York scratched his bearded chin. "Well, my prisoner says the gang is hidden out in a ghost town around here somewheres. In the hills, the mountains. But that's all he claims to know."

The mercantile man and the hardware-store owner exchanged glances. What was that about?

York said, "My deputy says there are half a dozen ghost towns that are possibilities. But checking each one out would be a prolonged affair. Are you gents familiar with the ghost towns hereabouts?"

Nods came from around the table, Mathers saying, "Some, perhaps."

"Which one would be closest to where that stagecoach was taken?"

The hardware seller frowned in thought. He glanced at Harris, who frowned back at him.

Mathers ignored his fellow merchant's frown and said, "Hell Junction might make a starting point."

"Hell Junction?" York said, frowning. "There was a town around here that called itself *Hell* Junction?"

Shifting in his chair, his smile oddly sour, Mathers said, "Well, the actual name is 'Hale Junction.' But everybody started calling it 'Hell Junction,' when things starting going, well, to hell. Silver mine went bust. What separates it from the other ghost towns in the hills is that there's still a functioning hotel there."

York's frown deepened. "For what reason?"

Mathers lifted a shoulder. "I couldn't say. But I can tell you the way to get there. Give you good directions. You see, uh . . . I make a run, now and then, delivering various supplies. So do several other businesses here in Trinidad. And, now and then, Mr. Wiley, the owner of the Hale Junction Inn, brings in a buckboard for a load himself. Newt here has done business with him, as well. Haven't you, Newt?"

The smile Harris gave his fellow merchant could not have been more forced. "I have, time to time. Never been to Hell Junction, personally," Harris said.

"Why in hell," York said, shuffling no longer, leaning in as if he were preparing to pull in a big pot, "would a hotel stay open in a damn ghost town?"

Harris and Mathers again exchanged looks—guilty looks, and the mayor and the druggist also gave the appearance of naughty children who'd been caught at the molasses.

Mathers, keeping his voice down, barely audible above the barroom noise, said, "I can't really say."

"Can't or won't?" York's upper teeth were showing. "Mr. Mathers, the lives of Raymond Parker, Willa Cullen, and Rita Filley hang in the balance. You do not want to know the lengths to which I would go to get this information out of you. So you damn well will give it to me. Now."

The city fathers made one collective gulp, an almost comical sight, though it did not make York smile, much less laugh. But finally it was Mathers who made the admission.

"The hotel at Hell Junction," he said, "is a place in this part of the world where folks can stay a while . . . no questions asked. *If* they pay the going rate. Or such is the rumor, at least."

York, seething, got to his feet, his chair legs scraping, screeching.

"You mean to say, gentlemen, that there's a place in this part of the world—in *my* county—where an outlaw can get away from it all? Where a killer can go to hell and like it? And no one thought to tell me about it?"

Sighs were followed by chagrined nods.

"I appreciate the information, gents," he said. "You'll have to excuse me. Not in the mood for a game this evening."

Or their company.

And he went out into the night before he did something he'd regret. He had to cool down and he had to think.

But one thought he'd already had: the good folks of Trinidad liked doing business with Hell Junction. And as far as he was concerned, that made them accomplices in this damn thing.

CHAPTER SIX

Finding herself sharing a red-and-black brocade two-seater sofa with Willa Cullen was nothing Rita Filley could ever have contemplated.

That the sofa was well-worn and that the big windows to their backs onto the street were boarded over, the glass long since broken out and swept away, did not lessen the improbability of sitting with the Cullen girl in a hotel lobby. Granted, the Hale Junction Inn was in a ghost town whose silver strike had struck out; but the hotel itself was undeniably a going concern.

Rita had heard rumors of the hotel, and the words "Hell Junction" were known to her, also. But she was relatively new to the territory, having inherited the Victory Saloon from her late sister Lola, and—with the exception of Trinidad and its thriving neighbor, Las Vegas—she remained unfamiliar with much of New Mexico.

So where exactly Hell Junction might be was unknown to her.

On the other hand, that a hideout for men on the run existed somewhere in the hills and mountains, hugging the horizon north of Trinidad, was information she'd gathered without trying. A beautiful saloon owner in satin, wending her way through her establishment spreading smiles and encouraging spending, tended to pick such things up. She had not inquired as to details, as not all information was good to have. Her business depended on friendly relations with Caleb York, who would not look kindly on an outlaw resort.

Some things were better not to know.

But she knew enough now to understand the predicament she and her new friend, Willa Cullen, found themselves in. Did "friend" overstate it? Probably. But they were at least allies now, the saloon proprietress and this stuck-up female ranch owner; and chief among Rita's tasks here at the Hale Junction Inn was letting the girl know just how much trouble they both were in.

Specifically, that even if Parker's ransom got paid, the busisnessman might still die. And in any case, two disposable women likely would. Witnesses were unpopular with thieves turned murderers.

Parker had finally gathered himself, Rita could tell, even if outwardly he might appear much the same. A new alertness in his eyes, and the way he stealthily followed the actions of his captors while pretending to stare into space, indicated the big-city tycoon was reverting to the frontiersman he'd been years before, when he was partnered with the Cullen girl's late father, George.

Rita figured he was, to some degree, playing possum.

Meanwhile, Randy, the youngest of the outlaws, was looking after all three hostages. Juanita, Hargrave's bosomy *querida*, was off helping with the fallen gang member—Bemis, his name was. Right now, Randy was paying much more attention to Rita and her admittedly fetching companion than to the rich man they'd grabbed. The boy was milling around the lounge area, not exactly pacing, staying close to them, but betraying a nervousness, even a shyness, that Rita could read.

She smiled at the boy. "Why don't you settle yourself, Randy? Or is it Randall? Do you prefer that?"

Willa gave her a sharp glance.

Randy lowered his head, moving it side to side, and said, "Aw . . ." It was minus only the "shucks." The boy in the sleeve-gartered gray shirt came to a stop, his pistol in hand, hanging at his side, swinging a little, like a deadly pendulum; the thumb of his left hand was stuck in the corner of a front pocket of the buckskin-color pants. The toe of his right boot kicked at the faded carpet as if it were dirt.

What a muttonhead, Rita thought.

"Mr. Hargrave," Randy said, "told me, Keep an eye on you two ladies."

"Why not do that sitting down?" Rita said, her smile pursed, a kiss promising perhaps to happen. "You could even keep *both* eyes on us."

He showed her those teeth that were as yellow as his hair. "My ma used to call me Randall. 'Fore she died."

"It's a nice name."

"I druther you call me Randy. That's what friends and such calls me."

"Is that right? Are we friends now?"

The teeth disappeared but a smile remained, and his voice grew soft: "I don't hold nothin' against you, lady."

Rita arched an eyebrow, sent him half a smile. "Would you like to?"

He blushed. Damn near tomato red.

Willa was staring at her now, her mouth open.

Rita got to her feet. Randy looked at her, his mouth

open also, but he said nothing. Did not tell her to sit herself back down. He was like a snake hypnotized by a swami. She went over and got a straight-back chair from where it rested against the wall and she plunked the thing down in front of her and Willa. Much too close for the latter's liking, obviously.

Then Rita turned to her flabbergasted captor, gestured with an open hand, and said, "Take a load off, Randy, why don't you? We'll likely be here a while."

Then she returned to her seat beside Willa.

Randy glanced around nervously. Nobody else was in view, the other outlaws all behind that closed door near the stairs, tending to their fallen cohort. He swung to Parker, who sat quietly in his overstuffed chair to one side of the couch, nearer the fireplace. The boy gave him a "Just you try it" dirty look. Parker returned the look impassively.

Randy took breath in. Randy let breath out.

Then he seated himself delicately in the straight-back chair, sitting close enough to her that Rita could reach out and pat him on the knee, which she did.

"There's a good boy," she said, then sat back.

"Iffen you're bein' nice to me, to fool me," Randy said, forehead clenched, "you best take care. I ain't the muttonhead what some folks think."

That he'd honed in on her very thought caught her off-balance momentarily, but she quickly said, "I'm sure you aren't, Randy. Really, all I want is for you and I to be, in your words—friends."

He thought about that; it seemed to hurt a little.

Then he said, "Why for?"

She shrugged easily. "Maybe because the rest of your bunch don't . . . appeal to me."

He thought some more. "Mr. Hargrave is a handsome feller."

Rita made a face. "But he's *old*, Randy. Thirty-five if he's a day. And he's *taken*, isn't he? By that Mexican woman?"

"Miss Juanita is only half-Mex, though she looks full-blood, all right. Last name ain't Mexie at all—it's MacGregor. But she's *all* mean, so I dasn't go after him, t'were I you. Mr. Hargrave, I mean."

She shook her head. "Not my type."

"Your what?"

"My type. Not the sort of man who appeals to me."

He squinted at her. "What would? 'Peal to you?"

"Oh, I don't know. A yellow-haired fella, maybe, not too old. And I like brown eyes on a man."

"I got brown eyes and yaller hair."

"So you do."

Willa folded her arms and straightened, her chin crinkled, her eyes narrow, almost shut, as she looked past this distasteful display.

"We'uns ain't your friends," the boy reminded Rita.

"No, but you and *I* could be."

"We could?"

"*Your* friends may decide to get rid of us."

"You mean kill you two females."

"Yes."

"They ain't yet."

"That's true. But killing women is frowned upon in this part of the world, Randy, and they might have brought us here to do that evil thing in a more out-of-the-way place."

He thought about it. This thinking didn't seem to hurt so much.

"Well," Randy said, "I cain't go against the others."

"Are you sure? I told you I was of means."

"I don't know what 'means' means."

She leaned forward some. "It means I have money, Randy. Not as much as Mr. Parker here, but enough to make you happy. And I might find *other* ways to make you happy, too, Randy . . . if you help me."

He leaned forward and whispered, "Help you how?"

"*Young Randabaugh!*"

The two words could have rung through a theater all the way to the back row of the second balcony. The cry was accompanied by quick heavy footsteps coming across the check-in area of the lobby. The outlaw leader in black and ruffled white was striding toward them, handsome face set in a scowl.

Fists on his hips in a manner again recalling a buccaneer, Hargrave looked contemptuously down at the openmouthed boy and said, "Why don't you just sit on the woman's lap?"

"Uh . . . that's a liberty she might not cotton to, sir."

"No, she might not at that. Nor is it one I would 'cotton' to."

Hargrave backhanded the boy, then got behind him and pulled the chair back rudely three or four feet, jostling him. Randy swallowed and blinked back tears, the corner of his mouth trickling red.

Standing behind him, Hargrave placed a fatherly hand on the boy's shoulder, leaned in to speak softly into an ear. "You are *not* to *trifle* with the *guests.*" Then he looked at Rita, realizing that she had been seated directly before the young man. "Nor are *you* to trifle with *this* innocent, ladies."

Willa said acidly, "*I* haven't spoken to him."

"I believe you," Hargrave said, then gave Rita a wicked smile that said he saw right through her. To the boy, he said, " 'Some Cupid kills with arrows, some with traps.' "

Randy was frowning, shaking his head, not happy with his boss. "It's red injuns what kills with arrows."

Hargrave slapped him on the top of the head. "Go see if you can be helpful in the sickroom, lad. Do it now. I'll take over here, for the nonce."

"Yessir," he said, got up, and paddled off with his head down, crossing to the door to the Wiley quarters and disappearing within.

Hargrave turned the chair around and sat backward in it, for some kind of dramatic effect apparently. Rita considered him an ass . . . if a very dangerous one. And a person kicked in the head by an ass could be just as dead as one trampled by a thoroughbred steed.

Which wasn't Shakespeare, but pure Rita Filley.

"You lovely ladies," Hargrave said, with a sweeping hand gesture that tried to be casual, though he wasn't quite actor enough to sell it, "would be well-advised to keep to yourselves. Cause us no trouble and when Mr. Parker's friends pay the freight, we'll free you as well."

Innkeeper Wiley emerged from the door to his quarters and called over to Hargrave. "*A word, sir?*"

Hargrave rose, gave the two women a cautionary raised forefinger, then went to see what Wiley wanted.

Willa whispered harshly, "What in the world were you doing with that boy? He's dangerous!"

"They're all dangerous," Rita whispered back. "But we can use some friends among the natives. You get friendly with Hamlet."

Hargrave and Wiley ended their conversation, the innkeeper quickly returning to his quarters and the outlaw leader loping into the lounge area. But this time the actor did not sit in that chair, forward or backward or otherwise. Instead he perched on the arm of the two-seater sofa, next to Willa. Parker was taking this in, being careful to maintain his beaten-down manner.

The actor's arm slipped behind Willa, not touching her shoulders, just resting along the upper edge of the sofa's back.

"I must apologize for that young ruffian," he said, his words more for Willa than Rita. Really, *entirely* for Willa. . . .

"He doesn't know better," Willa said, "although some people *should*."

His mouth twitched with amusement. "Where were you educated, my dear?"

Willa frowned at the familiarity. "I was taught at home by my mother. She was educated back east, very well, and she passed it on to me."

"I would have thought you the product of a private school for girls," he said. "You display a cultured, even refined manner that, frankly, makes me miss the company I once kept."

Rita doubted that. Actors were rootless vagabonds who just knew how to be flowery and well, particularly when someone else had written the words. But they really weren't any better than . . . well, any better than a saloon-keeper.

Willa asked her host, "Why do you keep such low company now?"

His shrug was an elaborate thing. "I'm afraid that where I was once sought by the finest theaters in the United States and their territories, I am now wanted only by the representatives of so-called law and order."

"Does that have anything to do," Willa asked with quiet condescension, "with going around holding up stagecoaches?"

He grinned wickedly. "It does, and trains and banks. But it began with an impulse I could not control. Someone insulted me and I took his life. Then, in one fell swoop, as the Bard says, 'My life was forever changed.'"

"Why not demonstrate that some good still lives within you?" Willa said quietly; then she touched his hand, which rested near his lap as he sat on the sofa's arm. "Let my friend and me go. What use would two women be to desperate men like yourselves, anyway?"

Rita thought, *If she doesn't know . . .*

"Your gentleness beggars description," Hargrave said, and there was something tender in his expression. Perhaps Willa Cullen knew what she was doing after all!

"*Eres un cerdo asqueroso!*" a female voice called from across the lobby, where it echoed in the high ceiling.

Rita was Mexican enough to know what that meant— Hargrave was being called a swine. She smiled to herself.

The voluptuous dark-haired, dark-hued woman in the overflowing peasant dress was storming toward them, fists clenched, eyes blazing.

She was waving, in her right hand, a revolver. A .38, if Rita wasn't mistaken.

Hargrave slipped off the sofa arm and Juanita was right there on him, shoving him to one side with her free hand; she leaned in and grabbed Willa by an arm, still waving that revolver (a Lightning Colt with a pearl handle, Rita further noted), and shook her like she would a disobedient child. Then the woman's left hand shoved Willa against the sofa's cushioned back, and leaned way in, the attacker's face almost nose to nose with the captive's, the snout of the .38 revolver against Willa's right breast. Rita was impressed with Willa's stony-faced reaction.

White teeth flashed. "*Maldita pícara! Aléjate de mi hombre!*"

Then Hargrave grabbed the small, volatile woman by the arm and dragged her back kicking and screaming to the doorway near the stairs; she was still waving the revolver, like a payday cowboy in town looking for a window to shoot out. They stood there shouting at each other, the woman using Spanish, the man using profane English that had nothing to do with William Shakespeare.

Willa, breathing hard, turned to Rita, who was smiling, arms folded.

"Do you see now?" Rita said, sotto voce. "Make friends and sew discontent. And perhaps reap the rewards."

Parker said, quietly, "Good job, ladies."

They sat quietly for several hours, with no guard at all for a while, though Rita and her two companions in captivity knew there was nowhere for them to go.

They had discussed it briefly.

"No one's watching us," Willa said.

Rita said, "That *Indian* is—out on the porch, standing guard?"

Frowning in thought, Willa said, "Maybe we could get out the back way."

"Through the kitchen? Overtake Mrs. Wiley? Who we haven't even seen yet, so can hardly judge her mettle. Still—perhaps that's possible. And then what?"

Willa shrugged. "Just run into the hills and take cover until they give up and get out."

"Or until they find us."

Parker, who hadn't spoken a word in some time, said, "We don't know our way around this place. Once we're shown to our rooms, we can start taking stock. Keep track of the layout of this structure. If we make an escape, it will almost certainly have to be after dark."

"Agreed," Rita said.

The businessman sighed. "We must stay alert and keep an eye out for escape possibilities. But nothing hasty—these are desperate, violent men."

Willa was just starting to say something when Randy reappeared. He came slump-shouldered out of the door near the stairway, crossed the check-in area, and returned to his chair, which he positioned several additional feet away from his charges.

"You ain't to talk," he said sullenly, "not to one or t'other, nor to me. And I ain't to talk to you, neither. Mr. Hargrave ain't happy with me and I aim to get back in his good graces."

Then the boy sat in the chair with the pistol in his dangling right hand aimed at the floor, as were his eyes.

Rita felt she could overpower the lout, and get that gun . . . but then what? Shoot it out with Hargrave and the boy's brother, Reese? And that crazy half-Mexican woman with her Lightning Colt .38? Who was to say the Wileys weren't armed, as well?

And then there was Broken Knife out front. . . .

She kept playing it out in her mind, different ways; but she ran the Victory, after all, and knew damn well the house always won. Parker was right—after dark was best. Maybe they could even get to the stagecoach horses for a getaway. If the Indian maintained his position on the porch, the horses hitched out front were out of the running.

Facing the three seated hostages, beyond Randy and across the lobby's lounge, were the windowed doors onto the dining room, where a light-skinned black girl in her early twenties was efficiently setting tables with plates and silverware. The girl, whose mixed heritage was evident, was a slender lovely thing in a black dress and white apron and turban, her hair cropped short; she wore simple hoop earrings.

An evening meal was served early, around four p.m., as the outlaw gang apparently had not eaten since breakfast. Innkeeper Wiley came to collect them, his black vest and white shirt splotched here and there with still-damp blood from helping tend to the gunshot patient.

Then Randy led the hostages into the dining room and allowed the three "guests" to sit at a table for four by themselves. Several tables away, Hargrave and Juanita sat, young Randabaugh soon joining them.

At another table, separated by vacant ones, were innkeeper Wiley and a woman Rita took to be Wilmer's wife, Vera, a sour, skinny, gray-haired woman in a brown calico housedress. The apparent Mrs. Wiley may have been the one who "ran a tight ship," but not its galley, as she was not in an apron or doing the serving, which was left to the colored girl.

The scattering of remaining tables, covered with linen now, had also been set with plates and silverware, as if other guests might yet arrive. Perhaps some would, but Rita had a strong hunch the hotel had been bought out by the Hargrave gang. The odd, faint formality of those place settings made the dining room and its empty, set-for-dinner tables perfect for a ghost town, the chamber itself on the dingy side.

That the hotel was a going concern did not preclude it

from suffering the ignominy of dominating a dead town and serving an outlaw clientele. The tablecloths, the drapes too, were frayed, the carpet worn, the chairs creaky, and when serving bowls were delivered by Mahalia (as the housekeeper/assistant cook's name proved to be), they were chipped, as were the plates.

This truly was dinner in a haunted house, in the company of ghosts and ghouls, the latter unfortunately still among the living.

On the other hand, the food itself was edible, if no rival of the Trinidad House Hotel's fare. Apparently the Inn meant to treat its guests right, however shabby their pedigree. The serving bowls delivered by the handsome serving girl brimmed with pork and beans, beef stew, and biscuits with butter.

Everyone was about to start passing those bowls around when Reese Randabaugh came charging in, his blue army shirt damp in front from having blood spatter cleaned off. He threaded through the tables till he hovered at the side of Hargrave, who was helping himself to stew from a serving dish.

"Blaine," the older Randabaugh said, "Ben's took a awful bad turn for the worse."

Reese certainly resembled his brother, but his eyes were blue, not brown, if just as close-set; a natural family handsomeness had been roughened by more years than Randy's, apparently fairly hard ones.

"We stopped the bleeding," Hargrave said, spooning stew. "He's conscious. Seems far from breathing his last."

Reese was shaking his head. "Well, he's gone right loco, now—outa his damn skull. Ramblin', talkin' crazy-like. Called me his *mama*. Feller's got the fever bad, Blaine. We can't just stand around and let him expire."

" 'Our remedies oft in ourselves do lie,' " Hargrave said, citing Shakespeare while ladling out pork and beans.

Rita, hearing this, figured Hargrave was fine having one less accomplice with whom to share the ransom loot.

Reese was saying, "Ben's been with us from the start, Blaine. With us all the way. He's a good man. We should *do* somethin'."

Buttering a biscuit, Hargrave said, "And so we shall. Go forth. Seek a ministering angel."

"You want a *preacher*?"

"No. I want a doctor. Ride to Las Vegas and bring one back."

"Trinidad's closer."

"Yes, but we don't want to attract further attention there. And it's a small town, with a storied sheriff. Let us seek a physician in a larger locale. Less notice will be taken."

"Ben might die 'fore I get back."

Hargrave dragged half a biscuit through the stew. "If friend Bemis cannot survive till your return, I doubt he would see the morning, in any case."

Reese sighed. "You're probably right, Blaine."

Then the elder Randabaugh plopped down in the empty chair by his boss and grinned as he reached for the serving bowl of stew.

A frowning Hargrave caught him by the wrist. "What are you doing, Mr. Randabaugh?"

"Well . . . shouldn't I fill my stomach, 'fore I start a long trip by horseback?"

"Avail yourself of some jerky and make haste. You indicate time is of the essence. I take you at your word. Leave *now!*"

Reese stared at the bowl of stew in his hand as if it were

a heaping helping of injustice. Randy, at the same table, looked like he wanted to stick up for his brother, but didn't. As for the older Randabaugh, he only nodded, put down the bowl, and hustled dutifully out.

Conversation at Hargrave's table accompanied the meal, but Rita and her companions were far enough away not to be privy to the hushed exchanges. She couldn't help but wonder if their own fate was being determined over stew, beans, and biscuits.

When the meal was over, the serving girl returned with a pie in a pan and a spatula, and offered everyone a slice (it was apple), starting with Hargrave, who said yes and gave the young woman his practiced dazzling smile. Randy was looking on with admiring eyes, as well, and Rita didn't think that was about the pie.

Juanita reared like a horse spotting a rattler. "Must we be served by this *puta negra*? Do we not pay *precios altos para este terrible lugar?*"

Rita heard that, all right. The half-Mexican woman was complaining about being served by a black harlot in this high-priced hotel. Whether Juanita was wanting to feel superior to someone, or was merely jealous of the look Hargrave had granted the girl, Rita couldn't tell.

But she didn't mind. Discontent was discontent, whether Rita and Willa were spreading it or not.

Hargrave and Juanita were on their feet now, the actor cursing at his *querida* and she cursing back. Finally she slapped him, and it rang in the room, which went dead silent.

"Perhaps I deserved that," Hargrave said, and made a bowing gesture.

Juanita's chin came up and her upper lip curled into a contemptuous smile for her lover. "You deserved that and more."

The outlaw actor grabbed her by the wrist and hauled her from the room. Their footsteps going up the stairs to the second floor rang out almost as loud as that slap.

Willa swallowed, said quietly, "I guess he's skipping dessert."

Rita said, "Is he?"

CHAPTER SEVEN

By late afternoon, Caleb York had already had a hell of a day—starting with an ambushed stagecoach bearing the two women in the sheriff's life and a key figure in the future of Trinidad, who was also a good friend, which gave the foul deed a personal slant.

Going from there, York had shot one of the outlaws dead at the relay station, tricked another of the gang into giving up key information, and learned that the very city fathers who paid his monthly wages were aware of the sanctuary for badmen known as the Hale Junction Inn.

Make that Hell Junction Inn.

As he sat behind his heavy wood desk in his office in the adobe jailhouse—the miscreant in his custody having nothing else worthwhile to share, it seemed—York pondered what to do next. He knew where the ghost town was—the directions were simple enough, thanks to those city fathers complying, and the ride was one he could make in under an hour.

"But what the hell do I do now?" he muttered aloud.

In anticipation of his nightly rounds, Deputy Jonathan Tulley was at the wood-burning stove, brewing up a fresh batch of what he claimed was coffee. He assumed the sheriff's question was meant for him.

"You could round up a posse," Tulley offered, leaving the coffeepot bubbling and taking a seat at his scarred-up table. He began to gesture wildly. "Rush the damn place! Surround that hotel and—"

"Get the hostages killed," York finished flatly. "But I have to do *something*, because some damn fool killed the messenger, which means the ransom won't get paid."

Tulley frowned and blinked at him. "Well, *you* killed the messenger, Caleb."

"I knew what damn fool I meant, Tulley."

With a sound that was part grunt and part sigh, York got to his feet and walked back to the four-cell block. Burrell Crawley was sitting on his cot with his head in his hands, whimpering, the latest dose of laudanum fading some, apparently. York shook the bars, like *he* was the angry prisoner, and Crawley looked up from his cot, startled, black eyebrows climbing the forehead of the narrow, pockmarked face.

Louder than need be, York said, "How much did Hargrave plan to ask for Parker's return?"

Crawley's expression was that of a kid about to bust out crying. "He never *said*, Sheriff! Swear on my mama's grave. Didn't you go lookin' for Ned Clutter? He's the one could tell you!"

"Not now he can't."

"Why, Sheriff?"

"I killed him."

The prisoner's eyes widened; he didn't seem to know whether to be confused or scared out of his mind. Some of both seemed the end result.

"K-killed him . . . why would you do that? Thought you wanted to talk to him . . ."

York flipped a hand. "He drew down on me and I shot him. Out at the relay station, where I caught up with him. That leaves you."

"Leaves me to what?"

"Tell me what ransom Hargrave seeks."

"I *swear*, I don't know!"

York frowned at the prisoner. "You were in on a *kidnapping*, and you don't know what the *ransom* demand was?"

The prisoner got off the cot and came over, shaking his head, keeping some space between himself, the bars, and York on the other side.

Crawley said, "I know what Hargrave promised *me*—two thousand dollars. That's enough for me to go straight! Buy a little ranch or somethin'."

The only place Crawley was likely to go straight to was Hell.

York asked, "What were the other men promised?"

"We never talked about that. Weren't nobody's business but our own."

York summoned a smile. "No reason to hold back now, Burrell. The more you cooperate, the easier it'll go on you when this is over." The smile turned nasty. "If any of those hostages is killed, you'll swing for it as sure as if you squeezed the trigger yourself."

Crawley was gripping the bars now, his light blue eyes welling up. "I swear to God, I'd tell you more if I *knew* more! I wish I'd never met that dadblamed Blaine Hargrave!"

The prisoner returned to his cot and resumed sitting with his head in his hands. York left him there blubbering.

Settling himself on the edge of his desk, the sheriff was so desperate he started talking over the situation with Tulley.

"Suppose," he said to his deputy, "I ride out there myself and offer to broker the ransom with Parker's business associates."

"*What* would you break?"

"No, I mean I'd be the intermediary. The middleman. Take the ransom messenger's place."

Tulley's eyes disappeared into slits, and he pointed a stubby finger at York's chest. "Wearin' that *badge*?"

"Yes. Representing Trinidad. I mean, they likely know I'm sheriff here. Why *not* wear the badge?"

Tulley shrugged elaborately. "Well . . . mebbe 'cause it'd get a bullet in it afore you stepped offen your horse."

His deputy had a point.

York said, "I could ride out there and sneak into that hotel and do my best to get the women and Parker to safety through the back or out a window . . ."

Tulley held up a hand with its fingers splayed. "Our guest in cell number two says they is five of 'em in that hotel hideaway. Also a female, half-breed Mex, who is meaner than the menfolk, accordin' to Crawley."

York nodded. Shook his head. "And that doesn't count the couple running the place. No, if I sneaked in there, I might be more harm than help. If the shooting starts, who can say who'd be killed?"

"Might even be Caleb York."

"Might." He narrowed his eyes, trying to see a way. "Still, after dark . . . most everybody sleeping. . . . I might be dealing with one or two of the bastards at a time. Pick 'em off. Better than a posse, anyway. Better than walking right in and trying to parlay."

Tulley was shaking his head. "They is all bad ideas, Sheriff."

He scratched his bearded cheek. "Sometimes you have to go with the least-worst bet. Throwing in my cards is not an option."

Tulley was studying him. Really looking at him funny.

"What?" York asked.

Nodding to himself, the deputy got quickly to his feet and raised a finger like a buyer at a horse auction. "Might have me an i-dee."

An idea from Jonathan Tulley? Stranger things had happened.

The former desert rat scurried over and plucked a wanted poster off the wall behind his table, one of many such circulars, only a few of which bore the faces of the outlaws sought. Many had mostly writing. One of the illustrated posters was Tulley's selection.

He came over eagerly, like a child with a good report card. "Take a look at this, Sheriff."

The face on the wanted poster was a drawing, not a photograph, and might have been anybody with a well-trimmed beard and a lean hard look.

Seemed the man was Bret McCory, who was wanted for a train robbery in Oklahoma and a stagecoach hold-up in Arizona. Colorado wanted him for the back-shooting murder of a marshal. No one wanted him in New Mexico. The poster had been sent to county sheriffs like York as a courtesy and warning.

Despite the murder, McCory didn't bring a "Wanted Dead or Alive" reward, but a reward "on arrest and conviction." The prize—$500—was on the modest side, and it said, "Immediately Contact Nearest U.S. Marshal's Office."

Tulley's grin shone through his white beard like a picket fence in a snowbank. "Why don't Bret McCory check into that there Hell Junction hotel? *He's* a bandit, ain't he? That's who they *caters* to, don't they?"

York winced, shook his head skeptically. "Tulley, I'm fairly well known in the Southwest. . . ."

"Sure you are, by way of drawin's on dime novels and such. Never seen no photographs. When you rode into Trinidad, not all that long ago, did anybody say, 'Well, look who it is! The famous Caleb York!' "

"No," he admitted. In fact, he had stayed a stranger in town for some while before revealing his identity. "What do you think, Tulley? With this winter beard of mine, could I pass for an outlaw called McCory?"

"Only risk I see," Tulley said, "is if one of Hargrave's bunch ever rode with McCory. But he ain't been heard of in New Mexico, or we'd a knowed about it."

York studied the poster, then tossed it on his desk and strode back to the cell block again. Crawley was sleeping. York kicked the bars and scared him awake.

"Crawley! Another question for you."

The prisoner glanced back wide-eyed and rolled off the cot onto his feet. He stumbled over to the bars and clutched them again.

"Try my best to help, Sheriff."

Butter wouldn't melt.

"Is one of Hargrave's men called McCory? Bert or Bret or some such?"

Frowning, Crawley said, "Heard tell of a Bret McCory. He killed a marshal in Colorado. Never met the man."

"How long have you been riding with the Hargrave gang?"

"Nigh on two year. Pretty much from the start of

it. Afore that, Mr. Hargrave was play actin'." Crawley frowned. "Me sayin' I rode with him, that don't constitute a confession of past sins, do it?"

"Not as far as I'm concerned, Burrell. Your best hope for a future that doesn't include a rope is to tell me everything and anything you know about this current crime."

Crawley grinned. "And of course I ain't guilty of that, 'cause I been in Trinidad."

Murdering some poor cowhand.

"Never heard tell," York said, "of this McCory among the others in your bunch?"

"No, sir. Why?"

"You asking the questions now?"

Crawley shook his head. "Surely not."

York changed the subject: "You had supper, Burrell?"

"No. I ain't et all day. I was all doped on that happy juice the doc give me."

"We'll fix you up."

The jail had an arrangement with the café.

York returned to his office, got behind his desk, and Tulley came over, delivering a fresh cup of coffee. York had a sip; it was hot and . . . well, it was hot.

York said, quietly, to his deputy, "I want you to go with me on this little jaunt. Won't take much effort to find a deserted building across the way from that hotel. We can situate you and your shotgun in a window where you can take it all in."

"Like the sound, Sheriff. Like the sound."

"In the meantime, go over to the café and let them know we have a prisoner who'll be needing meals, starting with right now. Then go over to Harris Mercantile. Newt's likely closed, but pound on the second-floor door, up those stairs alongside the building. Tell him we need his older son to fill in as a deputy, as we'll be leaving Mr. Crawley behind. And have Newt round up some road vittles for you—jerky, pilot bread, hardtack. Take a water jug. This expedition may take a day or two. Also plenty of ammunition for that scattergun of yours. Box of cartridges for me, as well. .44 caliber."

Tulley had been nodding all through that.

"Then go over to my hotel room," York said. "The desk man knows to give you the key. Get my carpetbag out of the wardrobe. There's a gray Stetson, kind of beat up, on the upper shelf. Bring that, too."

Tulley was efficient, running all those errands in under half an hour, including delivering Lem Harris—a strapping boy who was dumb as a post but tough as the jerky his pappy sold. York gave the boy a deputy badge and simple instructions and entrusted him with a loaded rifle from the rack on the wall.

"I'll get Gert loaded up," Tulley said, meaning his mule, and headed out with his arms full of a sack of things from the mercantile.

York put the carpetbag on the desk, next to the Stetson his deputy brought him, and selected from the bottom desk drawer some spare clothes fit for riding the range— buckskin jacket, green santeen shirt, canvas trousers, old boots. His professional black apparel would not do. He was Bret McCory now.

Just another outlaw.

The shadows were long as Dr. Albert Miller rode in his rickety one-horse buckboard along the narrow rutted road out of Trinidad. The going was rougher even than usual for the doctor and his Missouri Fox Trotter, what with the muddy patches left by the brief but torrential rain of earlier that day. With the rain passed, it was cool for New Mexico and would be downright cold by the time he'd make it back from the Brentwood Junction relay station with Sheriff Caleb York's latest addition to Boot Hill.

Not that those the sheriff dispatched from this life didn't deserve the trip—York, to the doctor's way of thinking, was himself a surgeon of sorts, highly skilled at removing damaged or diseased parts infecting the community. The doc was on his way to pick up the remains of just the kind of unwanted man in Trinidad who, paradoxically enough, was also likely a wanted one.

Ned Clutter, the sheriff had said, the dead man's name was—one of those involved in this hijacking of the stagecoach bearing Raymond Parker, Willa Cullen, and Rita Filley. The doctor dearly hoped he would not meet any of those three good people in his capacity as Trinidad's unofficial coroner.

On his way to the relay station, the doctor made a brief stop at the Trinidad cemetery. He always took this small side trip, when he traveled that road, whether to visit a patient or collect a corpse. His wife, Mildred, was buried here in the shade of the lone mesquite tree, far too gentle a soul to inhabit a place the residents called Boot Hill.

He'd seen that she got a nice stone marker, with the words BELOVED WIFE AND MOTHER and 1835–1880. She'd died much too young, Millie had, and for several years after her passing, he had wedded himself to another: demon rum. His children came to visit from the East when he stopped answering their letters, and got him straightened around.

He felt lucky he hadn't lost his practice during those dark years. But he'd done his drinking evenings and into the night—the hours he'd once spent with Millie—and he had not fallen so far that he'd neglected the living in his care.

But what a bitter pill it was to swallow, his wife—less than fifty years of age!—dying in her sleep with no malady to be treated or symptoms to serve as a warning. The only solace, though not a small one, was that she had not suffered. In this hard country, suffering often accompanied death. And it always accompanied life.

True, she'd been slight of frame and prone to every cold or minor ailment that could be visited upon a person. Her body was frail but her spirit was strong, and she had raised a son and a daughter with love and dedication. She had endured the life of a doctor's wife, the terrible hours, the need for her husband to put others above her, their children, and himself.

And she had done it with good humor and loving ways.

As he stood with his hat in his hands, staring at the gravestone, he did not speak to her, as some did. Miller was, in his way, a man of science and he did not believe she was there in the ground. Only her bones. But this was still a place where he could visit the thought of her.

The pear-shaped little doctor in the rumpled brown shirt with a black string tie climbed up on the buckboard, got himself settled, shook the reins, and resumed his journey. A breeze riffled his thinning white hair. In the back of the buckboard rode a lidded wicker coffin, waiting to be filled. Also tagging along was his Gladstone bag, not that this "patient" would have any need of the services it implied. But Doc Miller didn't go anywhere without the tools of his trade. You never knew when someone might need you.

The doctor slowed the trotter as he neared the relay

station's cluster of shabby gray, weathereded structures—a barn with a stable, a corral where a dozen horses milled, and the main building itself, the latter with a hitching rail and an overhang roof shading its porch.

Doc Miller left the buckboard and the trotter parallel to the building. On the saggy porch a man in a derby was seated on a barrel, leaning back against the wall, small enough that his feet didn't reach the floor. He had a thick black mustache and his gray shirt bore black sleeve garters and several food stains, chili maybe, and the duck trousers were a light brown. His eyes were unblinking and Doc Miller—carrying his Gladstone bag for no reason but a habitual protectiveness of the valuable case—was starting up the handful of spongy steps before he realized this was the dead man he'd come here to haul.

Normally, gathered flies would have told the tale, but it was too cold out for that. As he headed for the saloon-style doors, Doc Miller glanced at his future passenger and realized those stains were blood, not chili. Pushing through the batwings, he found Irvin Fosler working with a bucket and mop, cursing to himself as he cleaned the floor near the bar.

Fosler, typically in a bartender's bow tie, white shirt, and apron over black trousers, had his own elaborate mustache. The relay man's plump wife, Maria, in a colorful peasant dress, also had a bucket—that this establishment owned two buckets for cleaning purposes seemed remarkable to the doctor—and was scrubbing the wall behind the counter. It looked fairly clean, though Doc Miller could guess what the mess had been.

Caleb York did not suffer fools.

"That's an unusual display out front, Mr. Fosler," Miller said. "You might at least hang a 'Good Eats' sign around the poor devil's neck."

Fosler spat tobacco juice on the floor, then mopped it up. "You can have him. Do you know how many men Caleb York has shot down in this here establishment?"

"I'm not really keeping track."

Fosler paused, thinking, obviously not sure himself. "Well, too damn many. You need my help loadin' this one up?"

"Please. He's a small fellow, but I have a bad back and no physician to attend me."

Fosler nodded, then looked at his work appraisingly. He seemed satisfied, and indeed only a faint pink tinge on the planking remained to suggest the blood that had been spilled there.

Maria was also finished at her work and she now turned to smile at their new customer.

"I have stew," she said. "I have beans and tortillas as well, señor doctor."

"Fix me up a generous serving, señora. And coffee."

"*Sí*, señor doctor."

Outside, Doc Miller got the wicker coffin out of the back of the buckboard and rather awkwardly carried it up the stairs. He and the relay-station man removed the late Ned Clutter's derby and placed him in the wicker basket more gently than necessary, and Doc Miller closed the lid over him. Fosler considered the derby, then put it on. The two impromptu pallbearers conveyed Clutter down the stairs and into the back of the buckboard, where the doc draped a tarpaulin over the wicker casket.

Back inside, Doc Miller sat at one of the tables and allowed himself to be served up by the smiling, rather pretty Maria, who seemed pleased with how her man looked in his new hat. The stew was hot and good, and the beans and tortillas made it a feast. The coffee was hot and good; strong, too—just what the doctor ordered.

He'd barely begun the meal, however, when a sturdy sort of thirty-some strode in. He was blond, slender in a wiry way, with close-set blue eyes, and had a rough look about him. Wore a faded-blue button-flap army shirt, denims, and muddy boots, and had on a rather shapeless gray cowboy hat, which he removed, as if there were some reason to be polite.

Fosler, his mop and bucket stowed, his new derby too, was behind the bar.

"You got food, mister?" the man asked the relay man.

"We do," Fosler said, and told him what.

"Get me some, and a beer. Is it cold?"

"No. But the food is hot. Beer's warm."

"Give me some anyway."

The doctor took all this in while seeming not to.

The young man did not take a seat at the counter, and when he approached Doc Miller, the medico thought perhaps the newcomer meant to join him.

But the new arrival just stood there, hat in hand, and asked, "What is that in back of your buggy?"

"It's a dead man in a wicker coffin."

The young man frowned, confused. "People get buried in them, do they?"

"No. It's strictly for transport. Coffins for burying are wood. Why don't you sit, sir, and join me?"

The young man smiled a little, apparently liking the "sir."

He said, "That there poke?" And pointed to the Gladstone bag sitting on the chair next to Dr. Miller.

"What about it, son?"

"Is you a sawbones?"

"I'm a doctor."

The young man grinned. "Good!" He pulled out a

chair without a Gladstone bag on it and joined the doctor. "I was sent to look for a doc. Figured I'd have to ride
all the way to Las Vegas to find one."

"We're closer to Trinidad."

"Oh, is that so? I ain't familiar. You from there?"

"Trinidad? Yes. Why do you need a doctor, son?"

He thought about that. "Uh, friend of mine got hisself
hurt. He's a cowboy, like me, and he got tossed from his
horse. Spurred him a mite too often, I reckon. His leg
looks to be busted."

"Oh dear. Well, perhaps I can help."

"It's a bit of a ride. Not terrible far, but . . . a bit."

Dr. Miller touched a napkin to his lips and pushed his
empty plate away. "Well, as long as it isn't *too* far, it
shouldn't take me long to attend to your friend. We'll
work up a makeshift splint for him, and give him something for his discomfort."

"His pain, you mean."

"Yes. But, as we discussed, I'm hauling a body and I
must get it back to Trinidad soon, before it begins getting
ripe. You can understand."

The young man's eyes widened and he nodded several
times. "Oh, I can. You ever smell a dead cow that's gone
ripe?"

"I have indeed."

"Well, it's too late for barbecue then, that's for damn
sure."

"Yes, it is."

Maria served the young man a plate of stew and beans
with tortillas. Fosler brought over the mug of beer. The
young man dug out some coins and paid up.

"A second helping, Maria," Dr. Miller said, "while I
wait."

"*Sí*, señor doctor."

Between gulping down bites, the young man said, "Lucky I stopped here for some chow, on my way to Las Vegas. I ran off lookin' for a doc without takin' time for supper. That's just the kind of friend I am."

The doctor's second helping arrived. "Glad you stopped here myself. This stew is mighty fine."

The young man grinned. "A feller has to eat."

Outside, in his wicker coffin, Ned Clutter—whom Randy Randabaugh had no notion was the corpse waiting for a side trip to Trinidad—wasn't hungry at all.

CHAPTER EIGHT

Few who encountered Juanita MacGregor were aware that her Spanish was so limited.

The twenty-four-year-old woman had been raised in a home where her late father had insisted that her Mexican mother speak English. When Papa was at work, her mother had used a mix of broken English and Spanish, which her daughter picked up. But the girl never became truly proficient.

Papa had a small but profitable business in Sante Fe as a wainwright, making and repairing wagons and carts. They had a little frame house in a mixed part of town, where white men could have dark wives and not get grief.

Juanita was one of four (the second child, the first girl), but at fourteen Mama passed, trying to bear child number five, the baby stillborn. After that, Juanita had to run the household, and Papa started in to drinking. He also began bothering her at night, stumbling in where she slept and getting in with her, calling her by her mother's name, and pawing at her. Before that went any further, Juanita lit out and the rest of the MacGregor brood were on their own.

Her voluptuous good looks—she blossomed early—led to jobs in cantinas in towns all over the Southwest, first serving food but later dancing, flouncing her skirt, and clicking castanets, traveling with several guitar players who had talented fingers. She married one such musician, a man whose name was Jacob and called himself José, but when she caught him diddling another dancer, she unleashed the invective in Spanish that she had picked up from her mother.

To this day, her limited Spanish consisted mostly of angry outbursts Mama had frequently unleashed on Papa.

Juanita had been dancing at a cantina in Tombstone when she met Blaine Hargrave, who took to her when first he saw her. He was appearing at the Bird Cage Theater, doing a Shakespeare recital. When they sat at a table in back, getting to know each other, and he found out her last name was MacGregor, he seemed greatly amused.

"Currently my best Shakespearean selections are from the Scottish play, my dear," he said. "Could it be I have found my Lady Macbeth at last?"

She began traveling with him. They did so in style, on stagecoaches and trains. She loved his voice, the rich way those fancy words rolled up out of his lovely, masculine chest. It was nice finding a man who could drink hard and never get mean, and could make love while drunk as well as sober. Perhaps better.

When that heckler in an audience in Abilene had called her man "a spic-loving ham" from the audience, she was proud that he'd stepped down from the stage, taken the offender's own gun from its holster, and shot him in the face, turning that ugliness into a mask of running red. No one ever stood up for her honor like that before.

Later she heard that the dead man had lost a bunch of

money to Blaine the evening before, and was going around saying the actor was a cheat, which took nothing away from what he'd done to defend her honor.

That of course was when their life as outlaws began, and it had been an exciting one, and most profitable. Blaine was gathering money for their future ("The world's mine oyster," he would say) and assured her their life as desperados was only temporary. Another year or two. He would open his own theater somewhere he was wanted only for his "thespian gifts" and not for his "peccadilloes," a word she loved the sound of and figured must mean "robberies."

They fought frequently, but it almost always stopped at yelling. He only slapped her now and then, much less than she did him, and while he'd raised a fist to her from time to time, he never struck her a blow. Always the cause of the battles was his wandering ways. She felt certain he loved her, but she knew his appetites were keen and ever-present. Yet she also knew when the look in his eye, for some wench or another, was serious and when it meant mere flirtation.

Their fighting was not all bad. It seemed to excite them both, and if she swore at him in Spanish, things got heated, in a good way.

Right now, in their spacious if dingy room on the second floor of the Inn, she was in bed smoking a cigarette she'd rolled herself. Blaine was next to her, smoking a cheroot. Their smoke mingled. Pillows were propped behind them. A small table on his side of the bed was home to a bottle of tequila and two glasses.

He poured a glass for her and then himself. The covers—rather threadbare, as was common in this hotel, whose upkeep was not in step with its rates—were gathered at both their waists. She had full, nicely rounded breasts that still perked, and she liked to keep them exposed in private, to further remind him what she had. And what *he* had.

How she loved his chest, with its black hairy nest for her fingers to wind in. He was so refined, with his fancy talk and continental flair; but was most of all a man.

Smoke streamed from her nostrils. She sipped tequila. "You will keep your hands off that blonde one, *cariño*, or someone will die."

He paused in his own drinking to turn toward her and give her a crinkly smile, as if his mustache were tickling him. "Someone? Would you murder *her* or *me*, my love?"

"She would die," Juanita said, matter-of-factly, and her right hand drifted to his chest and her fingers entwined themselves in the curls, then yanked a little. "I *might* spare *you*."

"That's a relief to hear you say."

Her hands drifted south and entwined themselves in other curls. "Of course, even spared, you might lose something precious to you."

Half of his upper lip curled, making a smirk out of the smile. Or perhaps a sneer. "If you refer to your sweet self, my dear, that would be tragic indeed. I would never find another leading lady so gifted."

She patted the part of him that had recently joined them. "Just keep your hands off *la perra*. Or your next performance will be in a tragedy."

He stroked her cheek. "You concern yourself for no reason, my love. I merely wish to calm the woman. To make her easier to handle."

"You better not handle her at all."

He laughed, sipped tequila, then rested the glass back

on the little bedside table. "We need to keep both those wenches at bay. When the ransom is paid, and Mr. Parker on his way back to his luxurious life, we'll dispose of both females."

She frowned, not following. "Dispose of in what way? Not set them *free*, you mean?"

One eyebrow arched. "Free them from their earthly woes. 'So wise so young, they say do never live long.' "

Now she followed. "Kill them."

"That's the standard interpretation."

Warmth flowed through her. Not passion—that was spent. Love. Sheer love for this man.

"A wise decision!" she said. "Dead witnesses are best." She leaned close, their breaths on each other's face. Quietly, but with some urgency, she said, "But why just the woman? Why not 'dispose' of the banker, too? Once we have the money. . . ."

He kissed her. Sweetly. Tenderly.

Then, their faces still close, noses nearly touching, he said, "Turning Parker loose . . . keeping our part of the bargain . . . that paves the way for the deed to be done again. If we slay him, my *querida*, people will not be inclined in future to pay a ransom for the return of a hostage."

She basked in this wisdom, then finished her tequila and passed him the glass, which he set next to his. She drew on her cigarette and exhaled smoke, which drifted wraith-like.

Nodding to herself, she said, "So you will wait till the banker has been delivered before killing *esas brujas*."

His handsome face settled into thoughtfulness. "Perhaps. Perhaps killing them in front of him would serve a useful purpose."

With no idea what that purpose might be, she said, "*Bueno* idea. Fine idea."

Seeming to sense her lack of understanding, he said, "It may prove helpful to let our male guest know of what we are capable. This may convince him to not come after us, or else face similar butchery."

A knock at the door interrupted.

"*What?*" Blaine called out, irritably.

"I'm back," came Reese's voice. "With a doc."

"Hmmm," Blaine said, more to himself than her. "That took less time than I imagined."

Her man got out of bed, wearing only long-john bottoms. He opened the door, and Reese stepped into the room. Annoyed, Juanita halfheartedly covered her breasts.

The narrow-eyed fool told Blaine about running into the doctor from Trinidad at the Brentwood Junction relay station, and how he got the doc to come along by telling him a cowboy with a broken leg needed attending.

Blaine listened to all that, then went over and started getting the rest of his clothes on, saying, "I'll be down momentarily."

But Reese, a shapeless cowboy hat in his hands, was lingering like a bad smell. "Listen, Blaine, I don't know what you decided about them two females, but gettin' rid of them might be a mistake. A bad one."

Had the dunderhead been listening at the door?

Blaine went over to him. "Is that so? And do you have a reason for forming this opinion?"

"Ain't no 'pinion. The doc and me had supper at the relay station, jawed some. Ol' boy tol' me all about how there was this stagecoach waylaid just down the road a piece. How this important businessman got himself grabbed, and two women passengers, as well."

"Is that so."

Reese leaned close to Blaine. "Do you know who those two women is?"

Blaine gestured dismissively. "No. They were simply along for the ride. They still are."

"That blonde woman is a big rancher," Reese said, eyes narrowing.

"That *woman* is?"

Reese nodded. "Her name is Cullen and her pappy died not long ago and left the damn whole spread to her. Biggest in the county. One of the biggest anywheres around here."

"Interesting."

"The other one, the dark-eyed lady? She runs the Victory Saloon. Hell, she *owns* the place! That's the only saloon in Trinidad, and one of the biggest, fanciest around. Gamblin' and girls and everything."

Blaine was nodding slowly.

"Seems to me," Reese said, smiling like a greedy child, "after we get Parker's ransom? We can collect on the womenfolk, too. They is surely worth more alive than dead, Blaine."

She hated the way Reese called his better "Blaine." There was something unsettling about it. Like the way he'd watched Blaine walk over in his drawers. Was the older Randabaugh some kind of Nancy boy?

As if catering to that, Blaine put a hand on Reese's shoulder. "You did well."

Reese grinned, then his expression turned serious again. He gestured toward the hall. "Best come down and talk to the doc. Ol' feller's pretty upset."

"Oh, is he now?"

"He seen the banker and the two women sittin' in the parlor and he figured out right away there weren't no cowboy with a busted leg waitin'. He's in lookin' at Ben right now."

"Go back down," Blaine said, with a flip of a wave. "I'll join you shortly."

Reese went out, closing the door behind him.

Blaine finished getting dressed, including strapping on (and tying down) his sidearm, then went to the door, paused to blow her a kiss, and strode out.

She washed up some, using the basin and pitcher and towels on the beat-up dresser, and then sat on the bed, brooding.

Juanita didn't give a damn how much the women were worth. But if that flaxen-haired hussy went after her man, there would be hell to pay.

After supper, Willa and Rita returned to the lobby and their two-seater sofa; Raymond Parker resumed his place in the big leather chair, as well. The trio had more privacy now, Randy Randabaugh a good distance away in the dining room, seated at a cleared table, playing solitaire. The windowed double doors were standing open so he could keep an eye on the captives. They could see him, too, cheating at the game.

Not long ago, Randy's older brother had burst in through the front, accompanying Doc Miller, of all people. The doctor was hauled in bodily, his Gladstone bag in hand, and he looked worried and confused, like someone rudely woken from a deep sleep.

But when he'd seen Willa and Rita installed in the parlor area, his expression became blank, a blankness that paradoxically said he knew at once where he was and what was going on. Reese hustled the portly little physician into the private quarters of the Wileys, where the wounded Hargrave gang member was being seen to.

Shortly thereafter Reese had rushed up the stairs, was gone for just a few minutes, then returned and disappeared back into the Wiley living quarters. The two women exchanged glances, then turned to Parker, their eyes asking him a thousand questions.

"I hope," Parker said, calm and steady now, keeping his voice low, "that the good doctor will be able to save his patient. I would not like to contemplate what might happen to him otherwise."

Rita said softly, "I'm not sure you're right, Mr. Parker. I'm inclined to think the great Blaine Hargrave would just as soon have one less reason to slice up the pie."

Parker's eyebrows flicked up and down. "A valid point."

Speak of the devil, Hargrave came quickly down those stairs and ducked inside the Wiley quarters. The quick movement seemed something from a French farce.

Glances between the hostages were again exchanged, but this time no words were spoken.

In a half an hour or so—though it felt much longer to Willa—Hargrave returned, dragging a frazzled-looking, askew-haired Miller along like an oversize child. The doctor's jacket was off, and his white shirt was splotched red; his string tie hung loose, like a dead snake, and he'd left his Gladstone bag behind, presumably near the wounded outlaw's bedside in the sickroom.

"All right, physician," Hargrave said, standing facing Miller, hovering over him in the middle of the outer lobby. "I heard what you told your patient. But what is your *real* prognosis?"

"I told him no lies," Doc Miller said, raising a palm as if taking the stand in court. "As you saw, I dug the bullet out successfully, with little fuss or excess damage to your . . . associate. He lost some blood, and he's weak, and I would not advise moving him tonight. Tomorrow, some time, or the day after, he may again be mobile. Certainly in a few days he'll still have some discomfort, but otherwise be right as rain."

"He passed out on you," Hargrave reminded the doctor.

Miller raised his other palm. "Yes, but that was the laudanum taking effect. I gave him a good dosage. He should sleep soundly and for a good long while."

"Do you feel he needs further doctoring?"

Willa could well imagine what was going through Doc Miller's mind. Hargrave was not about to release his latest guest, much less have him escorted back to Trinidad.

Rita whispered, "Doc's best bet is to stick around and stay needed. Otherwise the healer will most likely catch something incurable."

Miller, as if he'd overheard that, said, "If there's an available bed here for me, I perhaps should stay the night. If I am wrong about the patient's expected quick recovery . . . should he take a turn for the worse during the night, say . . . it might be prudent for me to be on hand to give aid."

Hargrave thought about that. Then, vaguely irritated, he said, "We'll find a bed for you."

The actor gestured toward the lobby's adjacent area. "Make yourself comfortable, Doctor. You almost certainly know my other guests, who are from your environs. You've eaten?"

"I have. At the relay station." He breathed deep, exhaled the same way. "But I am rather thirsty, sir."

"Coffee? Or something stronger?"

"Something stronger."

"They have whiskey and wine on offer."

"Wine would be soothing."

Hargrave's smile was perhaps not his most convincing performance. "Well, we *must* have you soothed, Doctor. I'll see to it."

Miller came in, exchanged wide-eyed looks with his friends, plucked a chair from along a wall, and sat himself near Parker, but angled so that the two women were also well in view.

Very quietly, the doctor told them of encountering Reese Randabaugh at the Brentwood Junction relay station, where the outlaw had lied to him about a cowboy with a busted leg.

"As soon as I realized we were heading into Hell Junction," Miller said, "I knew I'd been played a fool."

Willa asked, "You knew of Hell Junction?"

"Heard tell of it. My first visit, however. And I hope my last."

Parker said, "You may get that wish in a way you wouldn't relish."

"I may indeed." He was speaking so softly that Willa could barely hear him now. But she did hear him.

Every word.

Concisely, Miller told them that he'd been picking up the dead body of one Ned Clutter, the ransom messenger who, as it happened, Caleb York had killed this afternoon. That Clutter's corpse was in fact snugged in a wicker coffin right outside the hotel in Miller's buckboard, under a tarp.

Willa said, "Well, surely they don't know—"

"They *don't*," the doctor said. "And if they ever do, I

would likely be in even worse trouble than I am right now. So, I fear, would we all."

Parker, just as softly, said, "That means the ransom is *not* on its way."

"That's right," Miller said. "And our sheriff is beside himself for putting you . . . now, us . . . in that untenable position." He shrugged. "But apparently this Clutter drew down on him and our sheriff's well-honed instincts kicked in."

Rita said, "I don't mean to throw a damper on this lovely reunion, but as soon as Hamlet and the rest of his troupe realize no money's on the way . . . and that Caleb York *knows* about them . . . they are likely to drop the curtain and steal away."

Willa said, "Well, wouldn't you *like* to see these creatures disappear on us?"

Parker said, "Miss Cullen, without ransom money, we are no longer hostages."

"Exactly."

"But we *are* witnesses."

"And dead men, as they say," Rita said, "tell no tales. Women, too."

Willa felt as though she'd been struck a blow in the pit of her stomach.

"*Hey!*" Randy called, frowning over his cards. "You people over there—stop your talkin'! You're gonna get yourselves in trouble!"

Rita said, "I would hate for that to happen," loud enough for even Randy to hear.

The four guests of the Hargrave Gang followed the young lout's directive. They did not speak. They all sat with their eyes and their thoughts moving.

The colored girl came in and offered them wine from an unlabeled bottle on a tarnished silver tray with crystal glasses, two of which were chipped.

"It's a port," Mahalia said, with an accent that had some Texas in it. "Very sweet. Nice. You should like it."

They all accepted healthy glasses, thanked the girl, who nodded, smiled, left the bottle on a nearby table, and departed. She seemed sweet and nice, too. Certainly the wine was.

Hargrave's woman, Juanita, in her peasant dress, came down the stairs in no hurry, flashed them a dirty look, then entered the Wileys' quarters. A few minutes later she and Hargrave exited, and started back up the stairs, with her leading the way, tugging on his hand.

"Second dessert helping, maybe," Rita said softly with a smirk.

But when the front lobby doors opened, and a tall, trimly bearded figure stepped inside, shutting himself in, Hargrave and his woman froze on the stairs. Both were frowning.

Neither Willa nor Rita reacted in any noticeable way, although Willa's right hand and Rita's left found each other, tucked between them where they sat, and squeezed. Both the doctor and the businessman barely glanced at the new arrival.

All four hostages had done very well, as the man who approached the check-in desk and slammed his palm onto the reception bell, three times—*ding ding ding*—was Caleb York.

Though she recognized him at once, Willa was struck by how different he looked. He wore a fringed buckskin jacket that looked dusty and well-worn, dark green santeen shirt, brown canvas trousers, red bandanna tied around his neck, and scuffed-up work boots. In fact, the only item of apparel she recognized was the .44 Colt in its low-slung, tied-down holster.

Wilmer Wiley came rushing out from somewhere and got behind the check-in counter.

"Yes, sir," rasped the pudgy little man in wire-framed glasses, tugging his vest on, smiling obsequiously. "May I help you? Might I assume you know the nature of this establishment? And its rates?"

"I do," Caleb said.

From the stairs, a scowling Hargrave said, "Now wait one damn minute!" He came quickly down, like a swashbuckler who forgot his sword; of course, he hadn't forgotten his holstered revolver.

Meanwhile, the woman, dark hair brushing her shoulders, was leaning over the rail, smiling at the handsome stranger, some of her charms threatening to spill out.

Hargrave stood before Caleb—they were about the same height—and said, "My apologies for interrupting, my good man. But I'm afraid I have bought out the hotel for my party. I'm sure you'll find suitable lodging elsewhere."

"I've ridden some while . . . my good man," Caleb said, looking at Hargrave through dangerous slits. "I'm tired and I know who this shebang caters to. And I'm it."

Hearing this fuss, Reese Randabaugh emerged from the Wileys' quarters with a frowning Vera Wiley right behind. Randy heard the hullabaloo, too, in the dining room, and rushed out past Willa and the others to get in on it.

Hargrave's hand was hovering over his holstered

weapon. But so was Caleb's. They were staring at each other.

Reese yelled, "We got this whole place sewed up, mister!"

And Randy, moving around the edges like he was trying to hem everybody else in, said, "He's *right*, bud! Right now, we *own* this here place!"

"*Wrong!*" Vera Wiley screeched.

All the men winced, but Willa and Rita only smiled.

Pushing past the older Randabaugh, Mrs. Wiley got back behind the check-in counter and stood next to her husband, putting a hand on his shoulder, the first sign of affection between them.

Firmly, not at all screechily, the hatchet-faced woman said, "The Hale Junction Inn is a haven for poor outcast souls . . . them what can pay the freight, that is. Do you have one hundred dollars for a night's stay, wayfarer? Meals is included."

Caleb, still facing Hargrave, nodded. He dug in his left pocket and came back with a handful of coins, dropping them one at a time on the counter, five clinks. Even from where she sat, Willa could see the gold of them.

So could the Wileys.

"Double eagles," Rita whispered.

Twenty dollars each.

An eyebrow raised, Hargrave said, "I apologize for asking, but it's a necessary intrusion. Where did you get that kind of money, sir?"

"I made a withdrawal from the bank in Roswell," Caleb said, his smile a sideways thing that showed only a knife's edge of teeth.

"Posse on your trail?"

"No. I shook them. Led them on a merry chase, as Shakespeare said."

Hargrave frowned. "But he didn't say that."

"Somebody must have. Anyway, I heard it before. . . . Landlord, I could stand to eat. You did say meals came with my hundred dollars."

CHAPTER NINE

When he walked by Willa, Rita, and Parker in the parlor of the lobby, Caleb York gave them a glance, but nothing more. And to his pleasure and relief, none of them reacted to that glance or his presence in any way at all.

Sitting just inside the open doors of the dining room, the two Randabaugh brothers—that's who York assumed they were, at least, based on prisoner Crawley's descriptions—were playing two-handed poker for kitchen matches that appeared to represent actual money they expected to be receiving for their kidnapping efforts.

Reese, in a blue army shirt, and his brother Randy, in a homemade gray shirt with sleeve garters, were separated by perhaps eight years, though they shared the same straw-colored hair and close-set eyes that made them look dumb as a post. The major difference was the younger one looked even dumber, and the older one had blue eyes, the other brown.

York drifted by, not acknowledging them, taking a table at the far end of the dining room near a serving board. He set his hat and his .44 on the table, to the left and right of him respectively. He'd barely settled when an attractive colored girl of twenty or so, wearing servant's black, her hoop earrings swinging, came through the kitchen's push-style door with a plate of food.

She was the kind of mulatto gal some called high yellow, and gave Willa and Rita a run for the money as to who was the most beautiful female under this roof. Of course he had also noticed the pretty Mexican-looking girl leaning over the banister with her bosom on display and black gypsy hair brushing her shoulders. This Hell Junction Inn had no shortage of beautiful women.

Or of dangerous outlaws.

The plate of chow the colored girl bore looked good to York—stew and pork 'n' beans and buttered biscuits. She avoided his eyes as she put down the food before him.

York said, "Thank you, miss."

She looked up at him, surprised to be spoken to in such a manner. Her eyes were big and a bottomless brown. Very softly, in a musical way, she said, "You're most welcome, sir."

He held her eyes with his. "And what's your name?"

"Mahalia," she said, softly respectful, but risking a tiny, barely readable smile.

"Mahalia," he said, as if it were the first bite he was tasting, and it was delicious. "Lovely name."

She liked that. "We have wine and beer. Also coffee."

"Just a glass of water will do me for now. Maybe something stronger after. Thank you, Mahalia."

She nodded and went off, no more graceful than a fawn gliding through a forest.

From the table where the brothers were playing cards, Reese called out, "You like talkin' to niggers, mister?"

York turned and looked at the older Randabaugh. "Only people I dislike talking to are fools." Then he turned back to his plate, leaving the son of a bitch to think about whether or not he'd been insulted.

After that, York ate in relative silence, with no conversation coming from the parlor or from the two louts playing poker, but for the occasional, "Deal!" or "Damnit!" Yes, those matches were money.

The stew, beans, and biscuits were fine, and when York was done, the high-yellow gal brought him a plate with a piece of apple pie on it. She smiled less shyly now.

"You bake this, Mahalia?"

"Had a hand in it."

He took a bite. "Maybe that's why it's so sweet."

She smiled openly at that and damn near flounced off.

Caleb York, he said to himself, *you are still a devil with the ladies.*

He was amused knowing Rita and Willa would have witnessed this, even at a distance, and been given something else to think about for a minute or so besides their captivity.

He pushed his now empty pie plate aside, wondering what his next move should be, when the outlaw leader himself saved York the trouble, the actor's ambling stride announcing him with a flourish as he came across the room to York's table.

Hargrave was a handsome devil himself, a mustached rogue all in black, and was sending York a smile that spoke confidence while his tense eyes conveyed suspicion. He was carrying a bottle of wine in one hand and two glass goblets by their stems in the other.

The outlaw actor stood by the empty chair to York's left; he raised the wine bottle to shoulder level. "As the Bard says, 'Good company, good wine, good welcome, can make good people.'"

Good people. Right.

" 'The wine was red wine.' That's Dickens." York gestured for him to sit. "Join me. Pour us a glass."

Hargrave nodded in a half bow, a typically theatrical gesture. He was wearing his sidearm, its holster tie loose. The man sat, poured generously.

The two raised their glasses in a silent toast, then sipped and set the goblets sloshing down.

"You may have noticed," Hargrave said, "that the innkeeper did not ask you to sign the guest register."

York shrugged. "From what I hear about this establishment, that's no surprise. If there *were* names in that register, they'd likely be Smith or Jones."

Hargrave sipped wine. "Well-reasoned. And yet every alias has, lurking behind it, a real name."

"Real names don't matter much in the West. How many 'real' names did Billy the Kid go by?" York gulped some wine. "I hear Wild Bill's real Christian name was James. But nobody ever called him Wild Jim that I recall."

The actor's gaze was unblinking. "My name is Hargrave. Does that mean anything to you, sir?"

York nodded and nodded some more. "Certainly does. Famously trod the boards, did you not?"

Hargrave lowered his head and gestured with a little wave, in yet another near bow. "I did indeed. 'A poor player that struts and frets his hour upon the stage, and then is heard no more. . . .' "

" 'It is a tale told by an idiot," York said, finishing the quotation, "full of sound and fury, signifying nothing.' "

Hargrave's smile turned contemplative as he studied this dusty stranger. "So . . . you have in your lifetime read more than just the sentimental twaddle of Boz, hmmm?"

York grinned at him. "I also like Jules Verne, but not

enough to quote him. Wild yarns, though. You ever consider a journey to the center of the earth?"

Hargrave shook his head.

"We're all due such a journey," York noted, and had a sip of wine, "only not that far down."

The actor studied the newcomer as if York's face were covered in lines that needed memorizing. "You know my name, sir, but you haven't shared yours."

York served up another grin. "Didn't your 'Bard' say 'What's in a name?' Though as long and hard as I've been ridin', I doubt *I* smell as sweet as a rose."

The actor wasn't smiling now. "You have hidden depths, sir."

"Everyone in this place is hidin' *something* . . . sir. Including themselves."

Hargrave filled his chest with air, then let it out as he spoke: "I take it you've heard of my subsequent post-thespian endeavors? And of my associates?"

York flipped a hand. "You started out on one kind of poster, now you're on another." He raised a forefinger. "Me, I could only claim one variety."

Hargrave's eyes narrowed. "You make noises like a bounty hunter. *Are* you a bounty hunter, sir?"

York's eyes narrowed back at him. "Did you sit with me to hurl insults? Sir?"

The actor raised a palm. Shook his head, once. "No," he said. "But as I am not a stranger to you, it seems only equitable that you not be a stranger to me."

York pretended to think about that.

Then: "Name's McCory."

". . . *Bret* McCory, isn't it?"

York nodded.

Hargrave gave up half a smile. "You don't ride with a cast of characters, I understand."

"That's correct. I general do jobs solo . . . but if I need some backup, there's always one saddle tramp or another, in need of a dollar."

The actor's expression was languid, but his eyes were hard. "You hit that Roswell bank alone?"

"No. I had a friend." York patted the .44 on the table.

Hargrave's smile grew. "Such a friend one can depend on. Other friends less so, but I'm afraid I have rather . . . *grandiose* notions that make a touring company desirable. For the kind of productions I mount."

"You hold up trains. That takes men."

"It does."

"So do banks."

Hargrave's eyebrows flicked up and down. "Larger ones than Roswell, with a sizable retinue of guards, yes. No reflection on your accomplishment, sir."

"You also take down stagecoaches, I believe. And that takes more than a man or two."

"It does." Hargrave frowned to himself, drew a breath; he was thinking. Then he leaned slowly forward and said, in a stage whisper, "You may have noticed several guests in the parlor who do not appear typical of the lodgers regularly housed herein."

York threw a glance in that direction. "I saw 'em. They don't seem like fugitives of anything except maybe a Sunday service."

The half smile returned. "They did not check in at this hotel of their own volition. They are my guests—if unwilling ones."

York frowned in thought. "Hostages, you mean?"

"I do."

Wiggling a finger toward the parlor, York said, "That old boy in the fancy duds looks like money at that. What those women are wearing don't come cheap, either. Those are big city bought. Can't get them kinda goods from a catalogue."

"I would agree."

York pretended to think about it, then said, "Ransom, then."

Head back, eyes hooded, the handsome outlaw said, "Yes. Have you any ethical objection to abduction for profit?"

"I have no ethical objections to profit at all that spring to mind."

His smile broadened. "I can tell you, frankly, that there is potentially a great *deal* of profit to be made in this enterprise."

York squinted at him. "You've delivered the ransom demand to the old boy's people?"

Hargrave nodded. "I already dispatched one of my men."

I've already "dispatched" one of your men, too, York thought.

Then York said, quietly, "What about the women?"

Hargrave opened a hand and gave a little wave to the new comer. "There is a role *you* might play, if you are willing to join with me and my merry brood in the last act of our modest melodrama."

"I'm listening. Make your talk less fancy."

"Are you well known in Trinidad?"

"Never set foot."

"Do you realize you're within easy riding distance?"

"That so? And why the hell would I want to ride there?"

Hargrave leaned in. "To deliver a ransom demand for the two women. The fair one owns the biggest ranch in this part of the world. The dark-eyed wench runs the Victory Saloon, the largest drinking and gambling emporium around, I am told."

York frowned thoughtfully. "Who would I take the demands to?"

The actor sat back, made a throwaway gesture. "I haven't the slightest notion. Finding that out would be part of your job. Go over and make the acquaintance of those ladies and pretend to befriend them. Find out who in Trinidad cares about them—enough so to pay handsomely to see them remain among the living."

Now York leaned forward. "If somebody *does* pay, will these folks 'remain' that way?"

"What do you think?"

York made a clicking sound in his cheek. "I think butchering them two females would be a downright shame. A waste by men of what God so carefully crafted." He grunted. "It better pay damn good."

"I assure you it will. Go in there and befriend the unfortunates. As the Bard says, 'Friendship is a constant in all things.' "

York finished his wine in several gulps, lifted the empty glass, and said, " 'Wine is constant proof that God loves us and loves to see us happy' . . . Benjamin Franklin."

He set down the glass, got up, and ignored the frowns of Reese and Randy Randabaugh, as he drifted past the brothers into the parlor.

Again, the captives betrayed no expression of either concern or recognition as York approached and took the chair facing them, unaware he was filling a seat earlier taken by Randy Randabaugh.

Speaking very softly, York said, "The name you will hear me being called is Bret McCory. You probably already realize I am using an outlaw's identity to infiltrate this nest of thieves."

Parker, answering equally softly (as would the women in the conversation to come), said, "Can you be sure none of them know this McCory by sight? That none of them ever worked with him?"

"No."

All three hostages pulled air in. All three let it out, as coordinated as if planned.

"But," York said, "Hargrave knows *of*, but doesn't know *personally*, this fellow outlaw . . . unless he's a much better actor than I take him for."

Briefly York explained he'd been asked by Hargrave to "befriend" them. To pretend to sympathize with their plight and worm out of them the names of anyone in Trinidad who might pay a ransom for one or both of them.

Rita said, "So he knows who we are now."

"Not a bad thing," York said. "If you're worth money, it will help keep you alive."

Willa said, "Yes, but for how long?"

"Long enough for me to derail this runaway train. Anyway, we have a moment now where we can talk out in the open like this . . . softly, softly."

Parker asked, "Are there others with you?"

"Only my deputy, who is installed in a second-floor window across this ghost-town street. For when I . . . *we* . . . need him."

Willa asked, "No posse?"

"No posse. My judgment was, working this from the inside was a better strategy than bringing in harmed men on horseback and turning this into a siege. My goal is to get you people out of here, alive and undamaged."

"That will take killing," Parker said.

"It will. But we four should survive."

Willa made a face. "With the help of that old desert rat of yours?"

York's voice was firm: "Don't be unkind, Miss Cullen."

That lifted Willa's chin and widened her eyes—not at the term "unkind," but on hearing York call her "Miss Cullen."

Her expression told him that his remark had offended her, so he said, "You are 'Miss Cullen' to me here, and Raymond is 'Mr. Parker,' and Rita is 'Miss Filley.' "

She nodded, jerked back to reality.

York went on, addressing them all but looking at Willa. "Think back. You've seen Deputy Tulley reform into a man who can handle himself. You've seen him and his scattergun in action. In the streets of Trinidad."

"And," Rita put in, "at the Victory. Anyway, I agree, a general melee-style shoot-out could find the wrong people getting killed."

"Now," York said, "I'm still getting the lay of the land, here . . . and I have the aforementioned Mr. Tulley checking around the otherwise not bustling Hell Junction to make sure there are no lookouts positioned we don't know about."

"There's an Indian on the porch," Parker said. "His name is Broken Knife, if it matters."

"That he's on the porch matters," York said, "and I made notice of him coming in. He wears the jacket of a cavalry scout and the red turban of an Apache. Not a healthy combination for us."

Willa asked, "If there's no one stationed out back, however . . ."

Again York nodded. "It's my intention to liberate you good people tonight, with minimal fuss . . ."

"Gunplay," Rita said, redefining that.

". . . and threat to you. But first I have to know the geography of this building and of the outside surroundings before putting any kind of plan together."

"Cay . . ." Willa began.

"No," York said, stopping her.

She flushed.

Firmly he said, barely audible, "Unless we're behind closed doors, never call me by name. And probably better not even then. A slip could mean the death of us all."

She nodded, the flush fading.

York continued: "I'll tell Hargrave I introduced myself—that you have my name: Bret. If you must call me something, make it that. We are behind enemy lines—and have always to keep that in mind."

"Hard to forget," Willa breathed.

"Might I say," Parker said, "that I believe time is of the essence."

"It is indeed that. The longer we're here, the more likely it is some or all of us will be killed."

The female hostages exchanged grave looks. Parker was simply staring at York, but the businessman had a nice firmness about him, a tangible resolve.

"My hope," York said, "is to sneak the three of you out of here sometime this very night."

"Actually," Parker said, "it's *four* of us. Dr. Miller was brought here to attend an outlaw wounded in the hijacking."

"I misspoke," York said. "I'm aware the doctor is in, as they say."

Willa frowned. "How did you know that?"

York allowed himself a smile. "No great example of my deductive skills, Miss Cullen. The doc's buckboard and trotter are tied up out front."

The two women nodded at that.

"We overheard," Parker said, sitting forward, "that you had a run-in with the ransom messenger at the relay station."

"I did. A fatal one, where he was concerned. But he may yet deliver a message."

Rita's eyes narrowed. "I thought you killed him?"

"Certainly did. But as I approached the Inn, I spied a wicker casket partly covered by a tarp. And I believe I know who the passenger is, in back of that buckboard."

Judging by the lack of blood in the faces of the hostages, they all did.

"If he's discovered," Parker said, "our circumstances will change far for the worse."

York gestured with two open hands. "All the more reason to get you folks out of here sometime in the dead of night. If you'll forgive the expression."

The door to the Wileys' living quarters opened with wood slapping wood, and an individual stepped out— just the man the little group had been discussing, Dr. Albert Miller. The doc looked bedraggled and his clothing had patches of blood, both fresh and dried. He came quickly over, if stumbling a bit, into the parlor.

His eyes met with those of the seated York.

York saw confusion in those eyes, knowing the doc was trying to calculate exactly the meaning of the sheriff's presence. Simultaneously—also having heard that door open noisily, most likely—Blaine Hargrave came striding out through the dining room and met Miller almost directly in front of where York sat in the parlor.

Doing the best he could, what the doctor managed was a gesture toward York as he said, "And who is this then?"

York sprang to his feet and slapped Miller, hard.

The doc stood there, stunned, mouth open, eyes wide, some blood trickling from a corner of his lips.

Teeth bared, York grabbed the doc by the coat, shaking him like he would a disobedient child.

"You don't need to know," York said.

Then he tossed the doc to one side, with just a brief exchange of the eyes in which the two men understood each other and their respective positions.

Hargrave put a hand on Miller's shoulder and looked at York. "This is a doctor who's making a house call. We're grateful to him, but he is not one of ours." Then with a nod toward the three seated hostages, he asked, "Have you introduced yourself to our guests?"

"I said my name is Bret. And let's leave it at that."

"And Bret you shall be. But please do not damage the doctor—we have further need for him. Have you properly welcomed Mr. Parker and the lovely ladies?"

York nodded, then headed into the outer lobby, gesturing for Hargrave to follow. The outlaw leader frowned at being so summoned, but obeyed.

Whispering, York said, "They think I'm their bosom buddy. That just because I'm a desperate outlaw, it doesn't mean I want to see respectable people . . . lovely females in particular . . . abused and misused."

"Good. Very good."

York scratched his bearded chin. "They gave me several names to try. I believe it likely that these same city fathers will want their doctor back, so we may well have a fourth ransom to add to the kitty."

Liking the sound of that, nodding, Hargrave said, "Excellent. Might you ride now?"

York thought that over. "I suppose. But it'd be well into night by the time I got to Trinidad. Raising people

144 Mickey Spillane and Max Allan Collins

out of bed could stir a general commotion, I reckon. And nobody could get to the bank, should they need to withdraw money."

"What do you suggest? Wait until morning—'Tomorrow, and tomorrow, and tomorrow'?"

"I do. On top of everything, there's all this hard riding I had today—even a notorious bank robber needs his rest, y'know."

Hargrave smiled and nodded, seeing the sense of all that. "You'll head out first thing, then."

York nodded back. "Is there hay in that stable across the way? A stall maybe, for my gelding?"

"There is. We have the stagecoach and its horses stowed there. No one's guarding them, though, but my Indian, Broken Knife, has a view."

Conversationally, York asked, "What plans have you for that stagecoach?"

"None. Just getting it out of the way. The horses we can use to spell our own steeds when we hie to a safer clime."

"Good. I'll walk the gelding over and collect my saddlebags. With your blessin', I'll come back and head upstairs and see if my room has a comfortable bed."

Hargrave beamed. "You have my blessing indeed. Your sheets will be fresh and clean. This Mahalia is a wonder. And I might say I already find you a suitable, even commendable addition to our cast of players."

"Thanks. How's your man doin', the doc was tending?"

"I believe he's doing well. I'll discuss that with the doctor, when he himself is feeling better."

Miller had pulled over the chair that York had been using, where the plump little man now sat slumpshouldered, droopy-faced, thin white hair a wispy tangle, exhausted. He was trying to look dejected and fearful, too, but York knew the doc was relieved to find his lawman friend there, properly insinuated into the Hargrave gang . . . even though the doc's welcome had been a rough one.

Hargrave offered his hand.

Caleb York shook it.

Then the man calling himself McCory stepped out into a cool night onto the squeaky porch, wondering what the hell was next.

CHAPTER TEN

On the porch, down to the left a ways as York exited through the hotel's double doors, the compact Indian known as Broken Knife was sitting cross-legged, arms folded, chin on his chest. Apparently asleep . . . although York wouldn't bet on it. Next to the quiet but deeply breathing figure, a rifle across his lap, were an empty plate and cup—seemed the Indian had taken supper out here.

The figure didn't stir as York stepped across the creaky plank porch and down the equally noisy steps. But, again, the sheriff of Trinidad County would not have been surprised to turn and see eyes glittering at him in the dark, like a cougar studying its prey from the brush.

As York walked the crushed-rock, tumbleweed-touched Main Street of Hale Junction, moonlight washed the deserted mining town in blue-tinged ivory, giving everything an otherworldly glow. Wind gave a gentle ghostly howl, as if the dead were bored.

Out in front of the inn, to one side of the porch steps, some horses were tied up for easy access in case of an unwanted variety of visitors—a posse, perhaps, or a sheriff wearing a badge and not a false name. The doctor's buck-board with his trotter, still hitched up, was out front as well, parallel to the building on the other side of those steps. York was all too aware that the wicker coffin in back, draped with a tarp, held its own kind of hostage.

That none of the outlaws had thought to check the identity of Doc Miller's silent passenger was a blessing; but the possibility of that turning to a curse hung over everything.

For the next half hour York strolled Main Street, taking in the weathered façades of the theater where Hargrave had likely once performed, a general store, café, post office, saloon, assay office, and dead lumberyard, among others. He was a military man taking stock of a potential future battlefield.

On the side streets and two streets behind Main on either side were perfectly good houses, if paint-blistered and broken-windowed, their yards scruffy with weeds, echoes of the boisterous, growing community Hale Junction had not long ago been.

It was as if some plague out of the Middle Ages had hit, decimating the population and leaving their dwellings and businesses behind. How easily Trinidad could become such a place, if dire circumstances prevailed. York felt those who tried to keep the railroad out might have consigned Trinidad to a similar fate, but that bullet had been narrowly dodged. Fear of natural progress could be as deadly as the Black Death.

York returned to the hotel, where the Indian still apparently slept on the porch—the lawman collected the dappled gelding and walked it to the livery stable. There he found the stagecoach stowed away, as Hargrave had indicated, its Morgan horses in stalls. Gert, Tulley's mule, was in a stall here, too—obviously the old boy had done some scouting himself, and found the back way into the livery.

The man who wasn't Bret McCory fed hay to the gelding, then used those rear doors to skirt behind several buildings, winding up at the two-story structure whose bottom floor had once been the general store. The living quarters above, abandoned obviously, were accessible by an exposed stairway on the far side of the structure, not visible to the Indian on guard across the way, should the red man's slumber turn out to be faked.

After going in through what had been a kitchen, and crossing a hallway that cut the second floor in half, York entered a front parlor, where Tulley was seated near double windows that wore what little remained of its glass in jagged irregular teeth around the edges. Moonlight leached in, giving the desert-rat-turned-deputy and the area near the broken windows puddles of ivory to bask in on the street side of a room otherwise lost in darkness.

Unlike the Indian on the porch, Jonathan Tulley—scattergun across his lap, much as that ex-cavalry scout's rifle had been across his—was definitely asleep . . . unless the snoring the deputy was doing was worthy of an actor more skilled even than Blaine Hargrave. At least the sound of the logs Tulley was sawing didn't carry—York had walked past the general store and heard nothing.

The sheriff stepped gingerly into the darkness, but his boots announced him, crunching under their tread.

Tulley was instantly awake, jerking that shotgun and its twin black eyes up toward York, who said quietly, "It's me, Deputy. Lower that scattergun if you want your next paycheck."

Tulley's smile appeared in his beard like a blade glittering in the night. "You ain't much on sneakin' up on folks, is you, Caleb York?"

York knelt, his night vision with him enough now to see that Tulley had spread pebbles from the street all around the entry area into the room. Smiling, he rose and moved past the crunching little rocks that had exposed his presence. Then he crouched near Tulley by the windows onto Main.

"I tell people all the time," York said, "that they underestimate you. You took a look around, I see."

"How do ye know that?"

York brushed some dust and dirt away from the floor and sat by his deputy, his back against the wall.

"I figured," he said, "Gert didn't put herself in that stall. Come sunup, if nothing has transpired, you best move her back behind this building. There's trees back there where you can hitch her up."

Tulley nodded. "Best nobody from them lodgings 'crost the way should spy a strange mule amongst their familiar steeds."

"Right. But for now Gert's fine where she is." He gestured toward the street. "What did you see? Anyone standing guard or working the periphery?"

"Nossir. Jest that injun feller. He's small but big trouble, I reckon, iffen you should get on the wrong side of him."

"An ex-cavalry Apache scout? Yes. I'd wager he's the most dangerous one over there. But a couple of them are damned dumb, and nothing is more dangerous than an idiot with a gun."

"Ain't that the truth," Tulley said, nodding as he clutched the scattergun to him like a baby.

York almost grinned at that, but Tulley was no idiot—though the old boy was dangerous in his own right.

"Was that Doc Miller," Tulley asked, excited suddenly, his head bobbing toward the street, "I seen go up in there?"

York explained that the doctor had been brought here to deal with a wounded gang member, and also told his deputy about the wicker coffin the buckboard bore.

"Iffen somebody spies that dead feller," Tulley said, eyes wide, "we're gonna have a shootin' war upon us."

"We will at that. Only they're a regiment and we're a couple of spare troopers."

Tulley squinted at his boss. "What's your plan, Caleb? Knowin' you as I do, there *must* be a plan."

"Just the beginnings of one. All I really know is that the longer I wait to spring those hostages, the worse off we'll all be. Best we do this before morning, with the dark for a friend."

"No argyment."

York grimaced. "But I still haven't had an opportunity to get a handle on the layout of that damn place. Haven't even been upstairs yet. It's my intention, my hope, to find a back way out, and sneak those hostages free."

Tulley frowned in thought. "Where does I come in?"

York gestured with a thumb over his shoulder. "When I give you the signal, head down to the livery and hitch those horses up to that stagecoach. Go in those rear doors, of course. Keep the horses settled. Be nice and easy with 'em as you hitch 'em up. You don't want to attract any unwanted attention."

"Shore don't."

York shook a finger at his deputy. "Stay right there, sit tight and wait. If things get noisy across the way—gunfire, yelling—that'll tell you something went awry. Drive that coach up to the hotel, hell bent. I should be flying out of there with those folks."

"From around back?"

"Probably from in back, but I can't be sure. So when you bring that coach to a stop, position it between the hotel and its neighbor to the east. The assay office."

"Assay office, yessir."

"If you don't hear anything alerting you to trouble," York said, "just stay put there in the livery. It's possible I can make my way there with the hostages without alerting anybody."

"Iffen we take that coach down Main," Tulley reminded him, "they'll know we're leavin', all right."

York held up a cautionary palm. "If I'm able to sneak everybody out, we'll head over to the livery and meet you there, going in the back way. Willa Cullen is a skilled rider—she can go bareback on one of those Morgans. Parker knows how to ride and the Filley woman, too— maybe not expert, but good enough."

"What about the doc?"

"If Miller can't get to his buckboard, we'll need a horse for him, as well. He can muddle through a bareback ride, if need be. If we can sneak out on the street behind us, we won't be chased, not for a while anyway. But if they're on to us, we need the coach. And going down Main'll be the least of our worries. Got all that?"

Tulley was thinking. "Might be they's saddles somewhere in that livery."

"Might be. After you hitch those Morgans up to the coach, you can scout around for saddles and such. We need to be ready, a couple of ways."

Tulley's eyes were tight. "How outnumbered is we?"

"Well, there's Blaine and the two Randabaugh brothers. . . ."

"Is they the idjits?"

York nodded. "The wounded man, Bemis, may be up to joining the fray. The Apache, of course. Hargrave's woman is a hellfire Mexican gal. She'll wade in with the men, all right, bullet for bullet. The innkeeper, Wiley, has a business to protect, and his wife looks like she'd sooner kill you than look at you."

"But the menfolk only numbers five or mebbe six. That ain't no regiment, Caleb. And we's a two-man army, you ask me."

York put a hand on his deputy's shoulder. "You're not wrong, Jonathan Tulley."

The old boy grinned, and his eyes popped. "Got me an *i-dee*, Caleb!"

He grinned back. "The name's Bret McCory—which was also your 'i-dee'—but let's hear it."

Tulley's gaze was glittering. "Why not wait till all them outlaws is asleep, and you and me just go in and shoot 'em in their beds!"

That actually wasn't the worst idea Caleb York had ever heard.

"I believe," York said, "that damned Indian *never* sleeps. Or if he does, he's got pebbles scattered in his brain that start crunching when anybody approaches."

Tulley's face fell. "Hell, Caleb. Thought I had somethin' there."

"They are murderous kidnappers, my friend, and I would lose no sleep shooting them in theirs. But we are still just two men, and those outlaws will be spread out in three or more beds in three or more rooms, and that doesn't count the Apache on the porch. No, Deputy Tulley, we will have to find a more civilized way to send these sinners to Hell."

Tulley shrugged. "Anyways, we wouldn't want to kill that Mexie woman of Hargrave's. 'Taint right, killin' a woman in her sleep, all helpless and dreamin' like."

Again York put his hand on Tulley's shoulder. "Deputy, that woman is the first one I'd shoot."

Hearing that, Tulley's eyes went wide and his face seemed to turn as white as his beard. Or maybe it was just the moonlight.

Getting to his feet, York said, "I'm going to finally get the lay of the damn land over there—pinpoint who is in what room, see what kind of back way out we have. There's also a colored girl, a servant, who might be an ally. Might. We'll see."

"Shore is a lot of womenfolk over there."

"Yes. All very beautiful, and each in her own way . . . dangerous. Now, after I get a fix on the geography of that hotel, I will stroll back outside and roll myself a smoke. Just kind of take in the air."

Tulley grinned. "That be the *signal*, right?"

"Right. It's a signal that means two things—first, that I've found a back way out of that place. And second, that it's time for you to go over to the livery and hitch up that stagecoach."

Tulley's nods came quick. "And be ready to roll, should things go haywire, shootin' and screamin' and such."

"Shooting and screaming and such, yes. But with luck we won't need the coach."

Tulley squinted one eye. "But we'll need them horses, iffen your escape goes as quiet-like as you wish."

"Yes, but unhitching those animals won't take long,

and we need the option of you picking us up and creating a commotion, should, yes, the shooting and screaming start."

Tulley had kept nodding through all of that. He was raring.

"If you don't see me signal you," York said, "just sit tight, like I said. Tight and alert. You follow?"

"I foller."

"Deputy," York said, sighing the word, "four good friends of ours are counting on us. We have to stay sharp, and we have to be ready . . . for anything. And remember—we're here to free prisoners—not to take any."

That knife-blade grin came again. "Which is your way of sayin', kill them sons of bitches."

"Your eloquence is worthy of the Bard, Jonathan Tulley."

"Of who?"

"Not important," York said, gave his friend a smile, and went out, crunching pebbles.

The Apache on the porch continued his apparent sleep as York returned, having collected his saddlebags at the livery, where he'd entered from the rear and then exited out the front. Now he was coming up the hotel steps and across to the front doors with the usual creaking of wood beneath his boots.

The Indian did not stir.

York went in and was greeted by Mahalia, who flew from a chair near the check-in desk, apparently having been waiting for him. The lovely colored girl in the white turban dangled a key before him. Part of him wished it were hers.

But it proved to be his—1B.

"You be in the first room to the right," she said, gesturing toward the open stairs. Her apron was gone and the maid's uniform fit her trimly, hugging supple curves. She was very pretty, a mix of Africa and Europe, her complexion like milk chocolate.

Nice smile, too, as she said, "Two doors at the top is the inside privies. One for gentlemans and the other for ladies."

"This must have been quite a place in its prime," York said, taking the key from her with his right hand, his saddlebags slung over his left arm. "Separate baths. Indoor plumbing yet."

She nodded. "From a well outside, yes. I worked here back in them days. You could get a heated tub of firewood-warm water for fifty cents."

"That's not available now, I take it."

Her eyes widened a little. "I could do that for you, if you like. No charge."

"No. Thank you, though, Mahalia. Do they treat you right?"

"The guests?"

"The Wileys."

Her chin crinkled. "They works me pretty hard. But they pays me. Not much, but it's better than the plantation life my people knowed. I'm savin' up for *another* life."

"Good for you. Hide your treasure well."

"Sir?"

"Your 'guests' would steal the pennies from a dead man's eyes."

"That sure true, sir. That sure true."

He drew closer to her and quietly asked, "Are the women upstairs, and the older well-to-do gent—are they locked in their rooms?"

She nodded.

"Mahalia, could you spare a hairpin?"

"Sir?"

He dug in his pocket and brought back a gold eagle, then pressed the coin in her hand.

With another surreptitious look left and right, Mahalia plucked a pin from under her white turban. She gave the metal pin to York, who glanced at its two flexible prongs, one straight, the other ridged.

Just what he needed. All he needed now was a little information . . .

Very softly he asked her, "Which rooms are the unwilling guests in?"

He wasn't sure she would know what he meant, but she immediately did, her response barely audible. "The gentleman is in room 2B, he next to you. The ladies, they shares a room next door to his—3B."

"Where does Hargrave and his woman sleep? And those Randabaugh boys?"

She told him.

"What about that doctor?"

"Don't know. Never saw him come out from bein' in with the sick man."

He nodded slowly. Then: "And where do you sleep?"

Mahalia's eyes widened.

He grinned at her. "Nothing untoward. I just want to get a handle on my surroundings."

Nodding, she said, "I'm off the kitchen." Her expression said perhaps she wouldn't have *minded* something untoward from him. "I can show you around some."

"Please."

The living quarters of the Wileys were off-limits, of

course, but off the dining room, behind the front lobby, was the good-size kitchen, still redolent of tonight's good fare. Mahalia had a small bedroom—with little more than a cot and one tiny dresser—just off to one side. It had a door. The back exit was from the kitchen, directly at the rear of the building.

York asked, "Does anyone stand guard out there?"

Mahalia shook her head.

York opened the back door, which was unlocked. No porch awaited, just a few wooden steps. This was a street across which were the untended yards of dead houses, with another street of abandoned residences behind them, and woods beyond.

"That Indian," York said, "does he come around checking in back, from time to time?"

She shook her head again, but added, "Not that I ever seen."

He reached in his pocket for another gold eagle. Pressed it into the warmth of her palm. Her expression, smiling some, was warm, too.

"Sleep sound tonight," he told her. "Don't open your door unless someone comes pounding. *Really* pounding. Understood?"

"Understood, mister."

"These guests of yours . . . the *willing* ones . . . are very bad people. Even for the likes of this place. Stay well out of anything that might occur. Got that?"

"Gots it."

He gave her a smile and a nod.

She gave him a shy smile and a nod back, then slipped into her little bedroom, began to shut the door, hesitated, smiled again, not shyly, and shut herself in.

You have enough women in your life already, Caleb York, he told himself.

At the top of the stairs were the doors marked GENTLE-MEN and LADIES. Over to the left, on a chair leaned back in the corner, sat Randy Randabaugh, on guard but sleeping. Revolver in hand in his lap.

York unlocked 1B with his key and found a room that rivaled his own back at the Trinidad House. The bedclothes were a tad threadbare, the wallpaper getting faded, but otherwise this might have been any hotel in a town that was alive and well.

He tossed his saddlebags on the bed and returned to the hall.

Knocking gently on the door of 2B, he said, "Mr. Parker," softly, "Bret McCory. Sit tight."

York got the double-pronged hairpin from his pocket and pulled the pin apart, straightening it some. In the keyhole of 2B, he stuck the straight end in about a third of an inch, and applied enough pressure to bend the end of the pin into a hook. Then he placed the closed end of the pin about an inch into the keyhole and applied pressure downward until he had bent the pin ninety degrees.

Now he had his lock pick, and he used it.

"Try your door, Mr. Parker," York whispered.

Parker opened the door a crack, eyes narrowing at the sight of York standing there alone, and let his friend in. The businessman was still in his white shirt and trousers and shoes, divested only of his tie, vest, and coat. The man was, York was pleased to see, ready to travel.

"We can make it out of here," York said, skipping any preliminaries, "through the kitchen. Door opens onto the back. No porch. No guard."

Parker nodded, listening as York explained the plan to sneak over to the livery, where Tulley would be readying horses.

"Have you an extra gun?" Parker asked.

"I do, in my saddlebags, and I'll get it to you when we make our move." York did not want Parker armed now in case one of the outlaws checked on him, and got things started prematurely.

Parker was trembling in excitement, but also fear. "How soon do we go?"

"Damn soon." York bobbed his head toward the door. "The younger Randabaugh is on guard right now, in the hall. I'll take him out and then we'll just go down and out through the kitchen. Should be no fuss."

Parker frowned. "If you shoot that fool—"

"I'll pistol-whip him good. Likely kill him, which is fine by me."

"What of Willa? And Miss Filley?"

York gestured toward the door. "I'm going to fill them in now. I'll leave your door unlocked. But stay put."

Back in the hall, he knocked softly on 3B.

Rita's voice, irritated, said, "What is it?"

"Bret McCory," York whispered. "Hold on a minute."

Again he used his makeshift lock pick, glancing over at the slumbering Randy from time to time. Some rustling— of clothes, not cattle—came from within as he worked.

"Try your door," he said quietly.

Rita opened it halfway and York slipped in.

The two women had been sharing a big brass bed, which was enough to give a man ideas. The two females had been provided their luggage and both had availed themselves of dressing gowns—Willa in powder blue,

Rita in black-trimmed scarlet. Fitting in several ways, the colors telling a story, the gowns tied tight at the waist. The women's lovely faces, free of face paint, echoed each other with bright, brilliant smiles.

But it was Willa who threw herself into York's arms, hugging him tight. Over her shoulder, he gave a smirking Rita a shrugging expression, then held Willa out away from him.

"Very soon," he said, "I'm getting you out of here."

He told them how.

"When?" Rita asked.

He jerked a thumb at the door. "I just need to signal Tulley, across the way."

Willa asked, "Is everyone accounted for?"

"I think Doc Miller is within the living quarters of the innkeepers, as best I can tell. Randy is asleep in the hall, but he may be a light sleeper. And he's armed, of course. Hargrave and his woman are across the stairwell. The Randabaugh brothers share a room over there, as well. The Wileys and the wounded man are downstairs."

"And that Indian?" Rita asked. "Still on the porch?"

"Still on the porch. He's asleep too, but I think a bug passing wind could wake him. Excuse the crudity."

Willa smiled a little. "You're excused this once."

He raised his hands, palms high, as if somebody was sticking him up. "Just stay calm and alert. We're going out quietly, but things could get noisy."

They nodded. Willa hugged him again. Behind her, Rita blew him a smirky kiss.

Then York went downstairs, where all was quiet. Front lobby, parlor, dining room, kitchen with Mahalia's bedroom door closed—nobody, and nothing.

Satisfied, he went quietly out the front doors. The Apache seemed to slumber.

Good, he thought. *Let's keep it that way.*

York went down the porch stairs and stood near where the buckboard and the trotter were hitched up, and he got out the makings for a smoke, made one and lighted up, sucked in smoke, let smoke out. In nice full view of where Tulley could take him in from the perch above the empty general store.

Then the Indian was next to him.

The little Apache, the rifle held in one tight grip, only came to York's shoulders, but the man's dark-eyed look stood tall. "You go out earlier."

"So what?"

The silence of the night made a buzzing nearby seem louder than it was.

The Indian clutched York's arm and squinted at him, as if trying to bring the bigger man into focus. "Why you gone so long?"

"Just getting a feel for this place," York said. "I don't like surprises. And I *don't* like people putting their hands on me."

Then he shook the Indian's arm off.

The buzzing was building.

The Apache looked past York at the buckboard, where flies were gathering over the tarp-draped wicker coffin, like locusts looking to strip a field of its crops. The night was cool but not cold enough, it seemed, to keep the flies away.

The Indian strode past York and went over to the buckboard, where he leaned in, grabbed the tarp, and flipped it away. Then the hard little man in the blue cavalry coat climbed up there, as insects scattered, and opened the lid on the wicker coffin.

Looked in.

Standing high in back of the buckboard, Broken Knife looked down at York, who felt oddly small suddenly, and said, "No like surprises, too."

CHAPTER ELEVEN

Raymond L. Parker lay on his bed in room 2B at the Hale Junction Inn, in his shirt and trousers and even his shoes, his coat, vest, and tie draped over a chair nearby.

After Caleb York's instructions to stay alert and wait for their escape, Parker intended to be ready to check out of this establishment in short order. Elbows winged, propped up on two pillows, he was very much awake and even revitalized, despite this long and eventful day.

A man such as Parker, who wielded considerable power and controlled a good deal more of his destiny than the average man, was not suited to the helplessness of this situation. On the other hand, knowing Caleb York was here, worming his way into the good graces of these badmen, was one hell of a relief.

Parker did wish York had left him that spare weapon, but he knew the gunfighter-turned-lawman well enough to realize York too was an individual who liked to control his situation, particularly when it included the possible violent ramifications of this one.

As if putting a startling period at the end of that

thought, a gunshot rang out, loud as a clap of thunder, but coming from below, not above.

Much like waking from a nightmare, Parker jerked upright. Then he bolted from his bed and rushed into the hallway. Down to his left, the two women in their dressing gowns were emerging from their rooms, clearly shaken.

And over in his corner, Randy Randabaugh—rudely awakened by the gunshot—had sprung to his feet, his revolver aimed at the hostages, moving back and forth as if trying to pick out a target in a shooting gallery.

From a room across the way, the Mexican girl—a black silk robe hugging her voluptuous figure, her dark eyes wide and wild—burst from the room she shared with Hargrave. But there was no sign of the actor.

The woman bared her teeth and pointed across the stairwell at the prisoners. "What are *they* doing out of their rooms? *Qué tonta eres!*"

"I dunno, Miss Juanita," Randy said, lowering his eyes. "They musta heard that shot. Didn't *you* hear it?"

"Of course I heard it, you imbecile."

Hargrave's loud voice came up the stairwell, angry, shouting what must have been yet another Shakespearean quote: "*Of all the infections that the sun sucks up!*"

Juanita gestured impatiently over at the hostages. "March them downstairs! *Apúrate!* We need to see what the hell is going on."

Taking the woman's orders, the boy frowned at his charges and said, "*Git downstairs! Right now!*" The frown made his close-set eyes seem even more so.

Parker led the women down—this was one instance where "ladies first" seemed not to apply—and the young lout with the gun followed them, the gypsy-looking girl trailing after, muttering, "*Qué demonios . . .*"

What the businessman and the others saw, as they descended into the front lobby, was a dramatic tableau worthy of any stage production Blaine Hargrave might once have mounted.

The actor outlaw, in bright red long-johns and bare feet, was shaking Dr. Miller by his coat front, grasping the cloth in one fist, while in his other was a smoking revolver, pointed at the floor where a scorched hole in the carpet had been ripped by a bullet fired in anger. The plump little physician's glasses were askew, his wispy hair a fright wig.

Looking on with his back to the front doors, the Indian called Broken Knife stood, arms folded and expression stony. Leaning back against the check-in desk, Caleb York watched as if almost bored, hands on hips, casual but with his right hand near his holstered weapon. Between the Indian and the sheriff, just this side of the parlor, paced Reese Randabaugh, in his trousers and a white long-johns top, also taking in the scene, but seeming anything but bored.

The women remained on the stairs, each with a step of her own, the Mexican girl included, like audience members hugging the rail in a theater balcony, transfixed by the scene. Gun in the air, Randy slipped down the stairs behind them, clearly desperate to know what was going on, while Parker was already at the foot.

"What in God's name," the businessman demanded, "is going on here?"

Hargrave—in his red long underwear and with that demonic expression lacking only horns and pitchfork—glared over at Parker.

The actor asked, "How well do you know this man? This . . . physician?"

Staying calm, Parker said, "I know him well enough. He's Trinidad's town doctor. He also serves as its coroner."

Randy said, "Corner *what?*"

Apparently noticing the boy's presence for the first time, Hargrave released the doctor with a shove, sending him stumbling. Then Satan in long-johns went over to where Randy stood near the door to the Wileys' living quarters, though neither the innkeeper nor his wife had responded to the brouhaha, staying out of their guests' business.

As Hargrave took in the presence not only of Parker but of the women along the banister, he said gently, "How is it, my boy, that our guests are not ensconced in their rooms? Were you not entrusted with locking them in?"

Randy thought about that. "I, uh, thought I done so, Mr. Hargrave."

Hargrave slapped him, and the sound of it, in the high-ceilinged room with its open stairwell, rang out like a second gunshot.

The boy, his cheek instantly blazing red, lowered his chin and appeared to be trying not to cry.

Hargrave moved in a slow circle, addressing everyone in his audience. "There's a man I know, just outside there. One Ned Clutter. A friend of ours." Then directly to Parker he said, "The very friend, in fact, who we dispatched to Denver to acquire your ransom. Only he never got there, it seems. You see, he's quite dead."

The women on the stairs exchanged glances. So did the men below, with the exception of Caleb York, who moved quickly to Dr. Miller and grabbed the man by one arm and raised a fist as if to strike him a terrible blow.

"What *happened*, you damn quack?" York demanded. "Who killed that man?"

York's eyes were on Miller and Miller's eyes were on York. Parker knew that in the shared silence they had spoken to each other.

The doctor said, "Sheriff York shot him."

Hargrave closed in. "You witnessed this?"

"No! I am, as Mr. Parker said, the informal coroner of Trinidad County. The sheriff came to me and reported the incident, sent me out to pick up the body at the relay station. I told this man as much!"

The doctor pointed accusingly at the older Randabaugh.

Reese, somewhat changing the subject, said, "York made a name as a Wells Fargo detective. They say he brought wanted men back dead more often than living."

"Well," the doctor said, flustered but with his chin up, "he's sheriff of Trinidad now. And you best hope he doesn't track you down. Nobody's faster or deadlier with a handgun."

Only Parker and the two female hostages knew that the man of whom Dr. Miller spoke was standing right next to him.

"For what it's worth," the doctor added, "Sheriff York told me it was a fair fight. Your man made the mistake of pulling on him, it would seem."

Reese approached the outlaw actor. "Blaine, maybe we oughter light out, right now. I don't cotton to Caleb York and a bunch of deputies findin' us this close to home. And, like you said, our ransom demand never got where it was goin'."

Broken Knife, who thus far had added as much to the conversation as a cactus, spoke up. "If York come, we kill. Men come with him, we kill too. We have gun. We have hostage. Hotel . . . fort."

The younger Randabaugh, one cheek blushed bright pink from Hargrave's slap, said, "I'm with my brother. Iffen Ned Clutter is out there dead and drawin' flies, we ought put some distance 'tween us and that sheriff. Right damn quick."

"I second what Randy says," Reese said, then gestured to the hostages. "We just take Parker here and the women with us. We can use that buckboard, or the stage. Put some dust between us and York. Once we cross out of the territory over into Colorado, this York bastard can't even chase us no more."

From the stairs, Juanita said to Hargrave, "He speaks true, *querida*. It would not be this York's . . . what is the word?"

"Jurisdiction," Hargrave said softly, mulling it.

York stepped up and said, "Why are we afraid of one man, anyway? I'm new to this outfit, I know, but I got a right to speak my piece."

Reese scowled at York, pointed a finger at him. "You don't *git* a vote." Then to Hargrave: "I say we pack up and head outa here. Toss in our cards and take the game elsewheres."

Hargrave threw his red arms in the air, as if he were the one being robbed. This silenced the room. The arms came down. He wheeled slowly as he spoke, making sure his entire audience took it in.

"Is there any reason," he said in that resonant, trained voice, "to think this Caleb York would come looking for the doctor—or indeed *any* of us—here at Hell Junction?"

Looks were exchanged among the outlaws, "Bret McCory" included. Slowly, one by one, they shook their heads.

"That," Hargrave said, "is an opinion I share. We will stay. We will take what comes."

That was met with silence, not applause. But no further argument ensued.

The outlaw actor turned his gaze on York. "I'm afraid our young fool Randabaugh cannot be trusted with a simple task. The master key is behind the check-in desk." He indicated the wall of keys. "Get it."

York went back there and did so.

"Make sure," Hargrave said, "our honored guests are tucked in and locked away for the remainder of the night. Then come back down, Bret my good man, and we'll talk. I have something in mind for you."

"All right," York said with a shrug.

Hargrave spoke to the assembly. "In a few hours it will be dawn. Now back to bed, all of you!" He turned to Randy, who looked more hurt by the slight than the slap. " 'Asses are made to bear, and so are you.' Resume your post."

Addressing Parker and the women, Randy yelled, "All right, you people! Git back upstairs!" This he delivered with an authority that he didn't seem to buy himself.

York followed them up, a shaky Randy getting back into his corner but staying on his feet, holding his gun on everybody.

"Bret McCory" locked the women in their rooms first and then bid Parker enter his, whispering, "I *am* locking this, but I'll hold onto the key."

As reassuring as that was, the lock clicking, as the businessman faced that closed door, had an ominous sound.

Blaine Hargrave—born Benjamin Harper in Paterson, New Jersey, son of a gambler and a seamstress—created for himself a British background, after deserting from the 28th Massachusetts Volunteer Infantry Regiment during the War Between the States. The Hargrave name came from a Boston boy who had died at Fredericksburg of a bullet in the head, right beside Harper at the time, prompting his decision to flee.

Hargrave's trace of an English accent, and likely his rogue ways, he'd picked up from his papa, who had been run out of London long before Blaine's birth. His mother, born in New Jersey, was as literate as the family was intermittently poor, and had steeped in her son a love of Shakespeare, while making him feel special and gifted.

Which, of course, he was.

For a dozen years Hargrave was among New York theater's most successful, celebrated actors. His roles included Hamlet, King Lear, Macbeth, Shylock, and Richard III, and his conquests included numerous actresses, but more significantly the wives of several theatrical producers, which had led to his banishment from the Broadway boards, followed by the life of a traveling player, largely in the American West.

That life, as it happened, had appealed to him. He had picked up the tricks of a card sharp from his late father—shot to death at a poker table when Blaine was sixteen—and, often in the same saloons where he performed in various Shakespearean productions, Hargrave would add to his thespian earnings with poker winnings.

The man, who had interrupted a performance with admittedly true accusations about Hargrave cheating at cards, had peppered his heckling with aspersions cast upon Blaine's dusky female companion and, worse, his acting abilities.

The Hargrave flair for the dramatic had led to killing the man with his own gun, right there toward the front of the audience. The actor had known almost at once that this performance would be his most memorable, and it heralded a new chapter in a tempestuous life. He had been born to the stage. Now he was robbing them.

He felt the role of road agent was a temporary detour on his path, if an exciting, often exhilarating one. Kidnapping the Denver businessman would bring considerable booty, which—added to what he'd already accumulated—put his ultimate goal in sight.

His intention was to establish a theater of his own, somewhere in Canada, where he could once again pursue his art. Extradition between the United States and its northern neighbor was rare, covering only murder and forgery. And the latter was not one of his skills, while he had never been formally charged with the former.

As he sat, deep in the night, in the Hale Junction Inn's parlor, on the two-seater sofa where earlier his two female hostages had perched, Hargrave pondered the problem that had unexpectedly arisen. Ned Clutter's death, while no terrible loss to Western civilization (in any sense), meant that no progress toward delivering a ransom demand had been made.

But he considered this setback to be a minor one, particularly since he'd had the good fortune of adding a new and most worthy cast member. This Bret McCory was

obviously made of sterner stuff than the scruffy spear carriers Hargrave had accumulated in his latest company of
traveling players.

But could Hargrave trust him? He must get a feel for
the man.

Out in the lobby, Bret McCory was coming down,
flicking a smile the actor's way.

Hargrave called out to him: "Join me! We have much
to discuss."

McCory, moving with grace and ease, came across to
the parlor. He looked around for a chair to pull over, but
Hargrave patted the cushion next to him.

"Sit, please."

McCory did, leaning an elbow against the armrest,
keeping some distance as he half-turned to look at Hargrave.

"Discuss away," he said.

"You have arrived," Hargrave said, launching right
into his soliloquy, "at a most opportune moment. Not
only have I lost a good man . . . *fairly* good man . . .
another of my bunch is wounded and momentarily of
limited use. This leaves me sitting here in this shabby
castle with hostages taken half a day ago or more, but
with no method or means at hand to seek the desired
ransom."

"A right mess," McCory said.

"Additionally, I'm told this Caleb York—a gunfighter
who calls himself a detective, and is now a lawman—was
responsible for the loss of that good man—"

"*Fairly* good," McCory put in.

Hargrave twitched a smile. "*Fairly* good man . . .
which means he may well be on our trail, although why

this York creature would think to look for us here escapes me."

"Some in Trinidad may know of this Inn. Though I doubt they'd tell a sheriff they were doing business with such an establishment."

"Yes, I doubt they would at that. What about this York?"

"Never met the man."

"No?"

McCory shifted on the sofa. "I hear he's a killer, though. This Reese of yours is right. When a poster says 'dead or alive,' York only sees that first word. So it's said."

"Sounds more bounty hunter than sheriff."

McCory shrugged a shoulder. "That's part of how these sheriffs make a living, collectin' rewards. Their actual pay is small potatoes."

"You think he's a threat, then?"

"Do I look like I'm trembling?" His head bobbed toward the porch. "Still . . . that Apache makes sense. We can defend this position, if need be. But you better fish or cut bait, where this ransom goes."

Hargrave sighed, nodded.

McCory said nothing for a while, then: "I have a suggestion."

"By all means, let's hear it."

And what this new man had to say had the actor smiling from the start. Blaine Hargrave finally had someone to ride with who had a brain to go along with a gun.

"Fetch him," Hargrave said.

McCory got up and crossed the front lobby and went back up the stairs. Not a minute had passed when he returned with Parker in the lead, a gun in his back. The newcomer nudged the businessman with the barrel of his .44 until the man was deposited before Hargrave. McCory holstered his weapon and stood alongside Parker.

His eyes on the prisoner, McCory said, "The ransom being asked for you is fifty thousand dollars. Will your associates pay up?"

The businessman drew in a breath and then let it out. "I believe they will. I am willing to give you a note, authorizing them to use my money."

Hargrave beamed. "Very good, sir. Your cooperation is to be commended. You can recommend who among your people should be approached?"

Glumly, Parker nodded.

"And in the note you write, you will instruct that no measures be taken against the messenger?"

Another nod. Firm.

Giving the businessman a narrow-eyed look, McCory said, "These two women you're traveling with—aren't they wealthy in their own right?"

Parker hesitated and McCory grabbed him by the arm, hard, and asked, "Well, aren't they?"

The businessman swallowed and nodded.

"Are they likely," McCory said, "to repay you, should you stand for their ransom? When this is over and they are home, safe and sound?"

Parker hesitated again, but McCory—still holding onto the man's arm—squeezed. Now the businessman, his face tight with pain, said, "They would! I'm sure they would."

McCory spoke through his teeth. "To the tune of another fifty?"

"Sir . . . that is a lot of money."

"Do I need a banker to tell me that? Would they . . . would *you* . . . stand for another fifty?"

Parker again took air in, let it out, but said, "Yes. I believe they would."

"And this Trinidad doctor? Miller, is it? He's probably worth something. Doctors make good money. Would he have, maybe, five thousand he could pay you back for?"

Hargrave was very pleased with this McCory. He had smarts and he was tough. And nicely nasty.

The businessman was nodding. "If Miller doesn't . . . if he can't, or if he refuses . . . I'd back him anyway. The little town needs him."

McCory released the businessman's arm, flinging it. Parker smoothed his sleeve, trying to reassemble his dignity.

"Okay," McCory said. "Now, we'll get you some writing materials and you'll fashion a letter to your most trusted business partner, authorizing a ransom of one-hundred-and-five thousand dollars. In cash, small bills."

Parker nodded, properly cowed.

"We'll work out the details of the exchange," McCory said, "with your associates."

"Yes, sir."

"Just make it clear—no law, no double-cross. Or they'll get you back in pieces. Understood?"

"Un-understood."

Smiling big, as if in response to a standing ovation, Hargrave said, "Thank you for your cooperation, sir. . . . Take him back upstairs, Mr. McCory."

The bank robber grabbed the businessman by the arm once more and hauled him away, crossing the front lobby and going up the stairs. Again the outlaw pressed the nose of a revolver in Parker's back.

McCory returned in perhaps two minutes and sat back down next to Hargrave.

"Well, Mr. Hargrave . . ."

"Blaine. Please."

"Blaine. And make it Bret. So we have four hostages and one ransom payment. I call that slick."

"I call it efficient," Hargrave said, still smiling. "I'll have you take pen and paper up to our friend in a bit."

Reese Randabaugh, wearing an almost comical scowl, was coming down the front lobby stairs. He strode over and he gazed with slitted eyes at McCory, seated next to Hargrave.

"What's the fuss, Blaine?" Reese asked, standing before Hargrave and his new friend. "People trompin' up and down the stairs like the place is on fire. What gives?"

Hargrave flipped a hand. "Not your concern, Reese. Merely making some arrangements involving the ransom payment."

The slitted eyes opened wide. Reese pointed at McCory. "What does *he* have to do with it?"

"Mr. McCory is with *us* now. He's going to deliver the ransom demand. He'll ride out in the morning, head to Las Vegas and catch a train to Denver. Does that answer all of your questions?"

"*No!* Why trust *him?*"

McCory sprang to his feet and moved in on Reese, going almost nose to nose with him. "Why *not* trust me?"

Reese reddened. "You back the hell off, mister! Right damn now!"

"Maybe we *do* need a little room at that."

McCory's hand was drifting over his holstered .44. And Reese was armed too, a .45 on his hip.

Hargrave rose and gently pushed the two men apart, saying, "Now, we're all friends here. We're all on the same side. Strange bedfellows, as it were."

Possibly very strange. Hargrave had long felt that under a veneer of toughness, Reese was suffering from unrequited love for the actor. Perhaps Reese didn't realize who and what exactly he was himself. But after many years among theatrical folk, Hargrave could tell.

"Reese," the actor said, turning the man by the shoulders till they were facing. "Now that you've slept some, I want you to stay down here in the lobby and keep an eye on things. I need to catch a few winks myself. Would you do that for me?"

"Well, of course, Blaine . . ."

He raised a forefinger. "We need to increase our watchfulness. I am going to take your brother off his second-floor post and move him to the kitchen, where we can keep an eye on our flank. Mr. McCory will in turn take Randy's place upstairs. Is that agreeable to you, Bret?"

McCory nodded. Reese frowned, looking a little hurt by the familiarity between his boss and the newcomer.

"Bret here will fetch your brother," Hargrave told the older Randabaugh, with a dismissive wave. "You take that parlor in the Wileys' rooms, with its view on the side street. Pull up a chair and keep an eye out. Visitors may come calling in the dead of night."

With a deep pathetic sigh, Reese nodded, and walked across the lobby, slump-shouldered, then disappeared within the innkeeper's living quarters.

Hargrave and McCory faced each other now. The former asked, "You've slept enough? Don't mind sitting watch?"

"Got a share of shut-eye. Don't mind at all. But one thing."

"Yes?"

An eyebrow went up. "Once I'm back, and we have that ransom in hand, we won't need these hostages."

Hargrave's mouth smiled but his forehead frowned. "Surely you can't mean we should kill the lot of them?"

McCory gave up only half a smile. "Why, Blaine? You got a likin' for live witnesses?"

And the new man ambled across the lobby and up the stairs, while Hargrave—somewhat stunned—tried to think of anything that was wrong about that suggestion.

CHAPTER TWELVE

When York reached the top of the stairs, the younger Randabaugh was already asleep in his chair in the corner, to the left of the indoor privies. The boy's head was lolled to one side, his arms hanging loose, but the .45 revolver dangling on his hip—its holster tie undone— would be deadly even in the hands of a dunce like this.

York went over and shook the boy by a shoulder, jerking him awake, Randy's close-set eyes leaping open, his hand dropping to his weapon. But York swatted the kid's arm away—not hard. No need to alienate him.

"Hargrave has a new post for you," York said.

Randy batted his eyes. ". . . huh?"

"He's in the parlor waiting with instructions."

The boy tasted his mouth, grimaced at the flavor, got to his feet, and went rattling down the stairs, stumbling once but catching himself.

Too bad, York thought. *If he broke his neck, he might save me some trouble. . . .*

The lawman sat down in the chair where Randy had been, and waited. In about fifteen minutes, Hargrave came up the stairs, his usual confident self. The actor ambled over to the seated York.

"Quiet?" Hargrave asked.

"Not a peep."

Hargrave heaved a sigh, half-smirked, his arms folded. " 'We have seen better days.' "

York grinned up at him. "That you or Shakespeare talkin'?"

"Both. We'll have a better day tomorrow. Riches await."

"Don't count Parker and his people out," York advised. " 'A rich man's wealth is his fortress.' "

Hargrave half-smiled. "That's not the Bard."

"No, it's the Bible."

Hargrave shrugged. "To each his own."

The outlaw leader walked down the corridor across the stairwell from the rooms of the hostages. He knocked at his own door and a smiling Juanita answered in a loose white nightgown, her breasts moving beneath the fabric like kittens playing in a sack. She threw her arms around him, as if they'd been apart for weeks. Hargrave kissed her the same way, put his hands on her waist and lifted her off her bare feet, then walked her in backward, using a heel to kick the door shut behind them. Lustful noises followed, including but not limited to bedsprings singing.

York waited it out. Silence came in ten minutes or so, but he took a good half hour before getting up and going over to knock lightly at 2B.

"Me," he told the door, and worked the master key in the lock and went in.

Parker met him, closing the door quietly behind them.

"We've caught some luck," York said, keeping his voice down. "I've replaced young Randabaugh as this floor's watchdog."

Parker spoke softly, too. "How did you manage that?"

"I didn't. Hargrave moved the dolt to the kitchen to stand guard at the back. There's some bad luck in that, too—Hargrave's increasing the guard everywhere, in anticipation of the legendary Caleb York coming."

Parker smiled, his first in a while. "They don't know he's already here."

"Thankfully, no," York said. "Those thieves took your watch off you, didn't they?"

"Yes. How on earth did you know that?"

"Never mind. Here's another. Thought one might come in handy for you." He passed it to Parker.

While a mildly puzzled Parker took the spare watch, York removed his own timepiece from his left-hand trouser pocket. "I have five after one."

"I'm closer to ten after."

"Set it back to jibe with mine. At four sharp, unless there's been gunfire or some other commotion, collect the women and come down to the kitchen. I'll leave the doors to these rooms unlocked."

Parker looked puzzled again. "Why would there be gunfire, Caleb?"

He pointed at the floor. "Randy is guarding the back door now, remember—which is our best escape route. I'm going in there and taking him out."

"Kill him?"

"Why, do you object?"

Parker grunted a laugh. "Kill him twice for all I care."

"I mean to pistol-whip him hard enough that he may never wake. I'll tie his hands behind him in case he does. But should I encounter trouble that I don't anticipate—

for example, should the Randabaugh kid be smarter than I think he is . . ."

"Which I doubt."

"As do I. But maybe he's tougher than I imagine, or perhaps someone will happen along while I'm dealing with him . . . in which case bullets will fly and you'll hear 'em. In that event, stay put and I'll collect you, if I survive. If I don't, your people will have to pay that ransom."

"Understood. But this bunch won't get the better of you, Caleb York."

"It could happen. An idiot killed Hickok, you know." He patted the businessman on the shoulder. "I'll alert the ladies."

York knocked at 3B, unlocked it, but didn't go in, whispering, "Are you decent, ladies?"

Rita appeared at the cracked door. "I would imagine that's a matter of opinion." Even without face paint, she was a pretty damn thing. Maybe prettier without it.

York slipped inside, shut himself in. Willa was standing near the bed, her expression keen and only touched with trouble. Both women were still in their waist-sashed dressing robes. He doubted either had been sleeping.

Very quickly, Rita said, "We've been talking, Caleb. We have a window . . ." She pointed at it. ". . . and can see a wooded area nearby, back there, beyond the empty houses. Why don't we tie together these bedclothes . . ."

"As a makeshift rope," Willa added.

". . . and you could be on the ground, armed and ready, and—"

Overwhelmed by the rush of words, York held his palms out in a "stop" motion, and softly said, "Much as I admire your ingenuity, ladies, and despite how it pleases me to see the two of you working so well together . . . the situation has changed."

He explained that Randy Randabaugh was watching the back door now, there in the kitchen. But he also told them he intended to "take care of" the boy and lead them to freedom without resorting to tying sheets and blankets together and risking a fall.

Rita smirked. "Now I wish I hadn't bothered buttering that boy up."

As Rita stood there facing him, with Willa coming up behind her, York said, "Do either of you have a timepiece?"

Neither did.

"No matter," he said. "Parker does, and he'll gather you at four a.m.—it's just past two now—and you three will sneak down to the kitchen and out with me."

Willa asked, "What about the doctor?"

"I haven't worked that out," York admitted. "We may have to leave him here on his own best devices. The gang has a wounded man and Miller's a doctor, after all. That may be enough to keep him alive."

Rita said, "You don't fool me, Caleb."

"I'm not trying to."

Her eyes were tight. "Yes you are. You'll get us out of here and have your deputy accompany us, then when once we're safely away, you will go back in here, gun blazing, to effect the doctor's rescue."

She was exactly right.

"No," he said. "I'll return with a posse."

Rita paused but then left it at that, though he doubted she really believed him. She surely knew that by the time he could escort them back to Trinidad and raise a posse and return, the Hargrave bunch would be long gone, either dragging the doc along or leaving him behind.

Dead.

"Do either of you," York asked, "have riding breeches along?"

Rita smirked. "For a clothes-buying spree in Denver? Not hardly."

Willa moved up next to the saloon owner. "I do. Several pair."

Rita gave her a funny look.

Willa gave Rita a funny look right back, saying to her, "I like to go riding. It's beautiful country there. Some of us see the West for more than a place to make money off the weaknesses of men."

Rita's expression clearly said the other female was a lunatic, and appeared to be looking for just the right words to express that opinion, so York thought he'd better settle them some.

"You two need to keep getting along," he said. "You can wait till we're back in Trinidad before goin' all catty again."

That made both girls smile. They, too, hadn't smiled much lately, and even embarrassed smiles were better than none at all.

York asked Willa, "Will a pair of those breeches fit Miss Filley?"

But it was Rita who answered. "They should. We're built about the same."

For some reason that sent red to Willa's cheeks.

"Good," York said. "Get into them. Match 'em up with shirts that aren't frilly. You must have brought some of your plaid shirts along, Willa, if you were planning to ride the mountain trails."

Rita was smiling, Willa still blushing.

"I brought two," Willa said. "She's heavier up top than me, but I can always sew new buttons on."

Rita giggled at that, and then so did Willa.

How had he come to find himself in the middle of this hen party? Of course, replacing Randy on watch up here made him the fox guarding the chickens.

"Get into the shirts and breeches," he told them, "but put those robes back on over them, and roll up the pant legs so they don't show. Should you be seen, for some reason, before we make our break for it, the suggestion of sleep attire could save your lives."

The women exchanged serious looks, then both nodded at York.

That was when the scream came.

They all heard it, a woman's scream, and two more like it, though the sound was muffled, coming from below.

"Sit tight," he told them, and rushed out, Rita closing the door behind him.

As he came down the stairs and into the lobby, the screams, interrupted by sobbing female entreaties—"*No! No! Stop! Please!*"—remained muffled but audible. Yet not loud enough that either Hargrave above or Reese Randabaugh at his new post was responding to them.

The screams came from the kitchen, where the only sign of Randy being posted here was an empty chair. Behind the closed door to Mahalia's room, however, came cries that were turning to whimpers.

York shouldered open the door and Randy, in pale yellow long-johns, was on top of Mahalia on her sad little cot, a child's thing on which a ripe woman lay, her off-white nightgown torn off the top of her, exposing creamy milk chocolate flesh, bursting with young beauty, her pretty face turned ugly by its contorted mouth and wide terrified eyes.

The attack was in its earliest stages, the boy holding her down with one hand and unbuttoning his long-johns with the other, or at least he had been until York burst in and the boy's hands froze on buttons nearing his waist. The brown-eyed face was blister white, eyes half-lidded, mouth hanging open like a trap door, drool trickling off the corners of his wet lips.

On the floor in the cubbyhole of a room were Randy's shirt and trousers and his gun belt. They implied a story: the younger Randabaugh had come into the room where Mahalia was sleeping; he undressed, not waking her, then stepped out of his things and climbed onto her and ripped her nightgown and her screams and terror began.

York came straight at the boy on the girl, but the boy beat him to it, lurching off the cot to leap at York, revealing quick reflexes that included flailing arms and hard fists. The impact sat York down, and suddenly he was the one under a boy whose swollen manhood tented his yellow drawers, already shrinking as its owner's priority shifted from lust to self-defense. Randy was pummeling at the man's chest when York's fist swung into the side of the boy's face with such power that it nearly tore the jaw off its hinges, and sent its owner toppling onto the floor on his side.

The young woman on the bed was sitting up, clutching bedsheets and blankets to herself, protectively, hiding her nearly compromised innocence but not her fear as her screams continued and accelerated, shrill in the small space.

York, on his feet now, kicked Randy in the side, re-
peatedly, boots digging deep, cracking ribs like celery
stalks, and now the boy was screaming too, but a com-
pletely different sort of scream. Picking him up by the
loose long-johns shirt, York thrust Randy against the
wall and banged his head into it, again and again and
again, dimpling faded wallpaper. He was still doing that,
even though the eyes in the boy's head had rolled back
into what must have been blessed unconsciousness, when
Reese Randabaugh appeared in the doorway, leaning in,
horrified, yelling, "*Stop! Goddamn you, stop!*"

York did, and turned, and Reese was coming at him,
fists ready, but the undercover sheriff whipped out the
.44 and thrust its snout in the angry brother's face, stopping him there in trembling fury.

Then suddenly Hargrave was in the doorway, his
hands leaning against the jambs, as casual as if he'd come
across a couple of fellows playing checkers.

"Gentlemen," the actor said, calm but firm, then came
over and up behind Reese to put a tight hand on his shoulder. "It would seem things have gotten out of hand."

Reese was seething, his brother an unconscious heap
on the floor, saliva and blood gathering at his open
mouth. Mahalia, sitting up on her little bed, had finally
stopped screaming, but she was shivering, as if a chill had
taken her, her face streaked with tears, the bedclothes still
clutched to her, the girl clinging to modesty in the shame
thrust upon her.

Reese could barely speak, but he managed. "Gonna . . .
gonna *kill* him . . . gonna *kill* you . . . bastard."

"You are welcome to try," York said coolly. "But your
brother was about to rape this girl."

"So what?" Reese spat. "She's just a nigger whore!"

York backhanded him.

Reese, blood trickling from a corner of his mouth, tried to wrest himself away from Hargrave, who was holding him from behind by the arms now. Tight.

"Let me go! Damnit, Blaine, let me go!"

"Let him go if you like," York said to Hargrave. "But it's cramped quarters for killing. Front lobby maybe?"

"Bastard . . . son of a bitch . . ."

"You're one bad name away from getting gut-shot. Keep it up."

"Boys!" Hargrave held firm to Reese's arms, whispering in his ear: "You need to settle yourself, friend. Your brother had a job to do and let himself be distracted. That endangered us all."

Reese was straining under the actor's grip, breathing hard, saying, "Maybe so, but he done *nothin'* to deserve *this* whooping!"

"Perhaps not. But your brother clearly doesn't understand the basics of life, such as one doesn't diddle one's cook without her blessing. You want hemlock in your soup?"

"I'll *kill* him, I tell you!"

"You do, and you and I are done."

Reese's breathing slowed; he stopped straining. Seemed to calm himself. Then he nodded.

Hargrave let go of him and the older brother went over and tended to the younger one, just a crumpled thing on the floor of the small space.

"What have you done, McCory?" Reese said, choking back tears as he knelt over the boy, glaring back at him.

"Well, I didn't kill the fool," York said. "Ribs heal. Might be concussed."

"Somebody get that damn doctor!"

Hargrave bent and patted Reese on the shoulder. "I'll see to it, my friend." The actor turned to the young woman, who was breathing slow, in the calm after her storm.

"My dear," Hargrave said to her, "there's a room upstairs I'd like you to make use of."

Juanita had appeared in the kitchen by now. Hargrave walked Mahalia to her, said, "Look after her, *querida*, but first bid the doctor join us here."

The gypsy-haired woman guided the younger female out, an arm around her, showing surprising tenderness. The blankets were draped around Mahalia's shoulders, squaw-like.

"Get back to your post, Mr. Randabaugh," Hargrave commanded Reese. "We should profit by the lesson of your brother giving over to distraction."

Reese sucked in air, glared at York, nodded to Hargrave, then collected the clothes his brother had dropped to the floor, gun belt included. He glanced one last time at Randy, and went out.

Hargrave and York were alone now in the servant girl's cubbyhole.

"Well," the actor said, "wasn't *that* unfortunate."

"Unfortunate that he was raping the girl, or that I stopped him?"

"You did the right thing. Your chivalry is to be commended, just as that lad's stupidity is to be abhorred. But I *need* my little crew, friend Bret. Now is *not* the time for the winter of our discontent. We need to band together."

"Yeah. I know. I just don't cotton to women being taken that way."

Hargrave put a hand on York's shoulder, squeezed in a gentle, friendly manner. With his other hand, the actor gestured vaguely to the world beyond the ghost-town hotel.

"Somewhere out there," Hargrave said, "this Caleb York is gathering the dogs of war against us. We must be ready. United." He shrugged, glanced at Randy, who was still unconscious, then whispered in York's ear: "But when all is said and done, only you and I need still be standing."

The doctor's voice came in before he did, as the plump little man made his way across the kitchen. "What's happened here?"

Doc Miller, in trousers and an unbuttoned shirt, Gladstone bag in hand, lumbered in, frowning as he paused to take in the pile of bones and flesh in long-johns slumped against the wall. He knelt and began his examination.

"I kicked him in the ribs, doctor," York said, helpfully. "On his left. Broke a couple, pretty sure."

"We can tape him up," Miller muttered. He glanced back with a scowl. "Are you people battering each *other* now?"

"The youth," Hargrave said, "was peckish but not for pie. He approached the cook, tried to serve himself a piece of a different sort, and Mr. McCory here took issue."

"*You* did this?" the doctor asked, as York knelt next to him.

"I did. In my defense, they stopped me. I was going to kill him. Rapists get on my bad side. Should've kicked him where he deserved it."

"Ah. A gentleman at heart."

Another voice came from the doorway: Broken Knife's.

"What?" the Indian asked, frowning at the crumpled, still unconscious Randy.

Hargrave walked him into the kitchen and explained what had gone on.

Meanwhile, York whispered to the doctor, filling him in on what was now his plan. A new plan, and perhaps not much of one at that. But the best he could come up with at short notice.

Hargrave was shooing Broken Knife back to his post on the porch when York came out of the little room and joined the outlaw leader in the kitchen.

"I should get back upstairs," York said. "Our guests seem to have slept through the merriment. But for all we know they could have taken advantage of the commotion to sneak out."

Hargrave only smiled. "I hardly think so. Still, go up and check, then stay on watch. With young Randabaugh out of action at present, I will assume the kitchen post myself."

"Seems prudent. All right with you if I stretch out on my bed, with the door open, should there be any mischief worth hearing?"

The actor shrugged. "Why not? Nap a little if you like. You asleep is worth ten wide-awake Randabaughs."

Soon York was upstairs, meeting first with Parker and then with the women. In both cases he explained that the inhabitants of the hotel were too awake, their hosts too alert, for York and the hostages to stage the escape as planned. Hargrave himself was on guard in the kitchen, a more formidable barrier than the boy would have been; and dawn was creeping up on them.

York used the same words with the women that he had with Parker.

"I have a plan," he said. "It's not without hazard, I admit. And I'm open to suggestion. It will be dangerous, but I will put myself in a position to protect you. All of you."

Then he told them what he wanted them to do.

CHAPTER THIRTEEN

York slept on top of the bed covers for almost two hours, in the Bret McCory wardrobe he'd arrived in, except for the fringed buckskin jacket, which he slung over a chair. Otherwise, even his boots stayed on, his .44 on the pillow next to his, the cold steel asleep on the softness of feathers—but ready to be woken, if need be.

But nothing disturbed his light slumber, and when York rose at 6:30 a.m., he used the nearby room marked GENTLEMEN, which had a sink with running water. Imagine—a ghost town hotel with such amenities. He splashed his face, dried it off with a towel, stuck his mouth under the spigot to wash the sleep from his mouth, and then looked at his bearded self in the mirror. Snugged on his battered gray Stetson. Nodded at his reflection.

He was ready.

A knock at 2B roused Parker quickly—perhaps the man hadn't slept at all, and though his face in the crack of the door seemed alert, the eyes were bloodshot. He too wore the same clothes as the day before.

"Got that ransom message ready?" York asked him.

"I do." Parker fetched it and handed it to the lawman, who looked it over.

York nodded at the page, then grinned as he folded it in thirds. "I like that extra five thousand for Doc Miller's end. Something about the hundred-and-five-thousand-dollar figure that makes it feel real."

"It does at that. Don't go running off with all that money now, Caleb."

"The name is Bret. Ready for what's ahead?"

"I will be."

"The women are your responsibility, here on out."

"We will be ready."

York's eyebrows went up. "Can't give you exactly when. But there'll be no mistaking when it's time for action."

Parker's expression grew grave. "Let's try to live through this . . . Bret."

"That's my intent." He tipped his hat to the businessman, who shut the door as York headed around and down the stairs.

Going directly to the kitchen, York found Hargrave seated at its small wooden table, where he was finishing off a plate of scrambled eggs and bacon. The cook this morning was not Mahalia, but Juanita, in another low-necked peasant dress, the black curls brushing mostly bare shoulders. She was at the stove cooking right now, the smell of bacon grease hanging heavy.

Hargrave said, "Good morning, Bret. We're allowing that poor child to sleep in—the girl the Randabaugh boy sought to ravage, I mean."

"White of you," York said with a nod.

Hargrave seemed spirited enough, but York figured the actor hadn't slept any more than he had—if that. The black clothes—vest, jacket, trousers, so similar to what

York usually wore himself—looked rumpled, the ruffled white shirt (*not* York's style) limp and wilted.

"Sit! Eat!" Hargrave demanded good-naturedly. "You have a long ride ahead, before you get to Las Vegas and a train with a dining car."

York sat and Juanita flounced over, ready with a plate of eggs and bacon for him, providing a nice view as she leaned in serving. Silverware was already waiting. So was a pitcher of hot coffee with metal cups. York poured himself some.

Hargrave was addressing his face with a napkin. York passed him the folded ransom message Parker had written. The actor read it, smiling wide. Somehow the mustache made that smile seem bigger and even more roguish.

"It would appear that the last act of our modest production," Hargrave said, "will end happily. And with the proceeds, I will no longer have to play the role of brigand."

"Why, what lies ahead for you?" York asked, keeping to himself his own ideas on that subject.

Hargrave wadded the napkin and dropped it on the table. Leaned back in his chair. " 'All the world's a stage,' the Bard says, but I intend to build a little world of my own, and become master of my own fate. A place where the dramatics in which I indulge will bring fame and fortune, not infamy and pursuit."

Between bites, York said, "That note is what you were after?"

"You read it. You do *read*, I trust?"

"Enough to get by. Seems fine to me. Parker's addressed it to a specific individual at his bank. His vice president. He put the address right there at the top, like a proper letter."

Hargrave was nodding. "An address that you should have no great difficulty finding. Have you been to Denver before?"

"I have. I know my way around some."

"Excellent. Here."

The actor handed the ransom note back to York, who tucked it in a pocket of the buckskin jacket.

The table could seat four. Juanita brought her own plate over and joined them; she began eating everything with a spoon. Her table manners were terrible, but the ferociousness of her approach somehow seemed consistent with her lustful nature. She would make a good woman for the right man. Unfortunately the man she had chosen was a wrong one.

"You need to make this transaction quickly," Hargrave said. "But don't make the mistake of expecting it to go smoothly. If they hand the money right over to you, they are fools."

"I doubt they're fools."

"As do I. So have this vice president accompany you with the money on the first train back to Las Vegas. He will no doubt insist on bringing along a bodyguard, a Pinkerton most likely. At Las Vegas, put them both on horses. Bring them to the rocky place at the bottom of the road to Hell Junction, where the pathways split off. Have them wait there. Ride in to town and I'll ride back out with you, with Mr. Parker in tow."

York nodded.

"Now," Hargrave said, "I'm afraid I'm going to disappoint you."

"Oh?"

He smirked humorlessly. "As much as I dislike witnesses myself, the breathing variety, that is, we simply must turn Mr. Parker over to his people. Otherwise, we would discourage payment in future such transactions, and who knows? I may need to make a guest out of some other rich bastard in the future."

Juanita paused in her gobbling to ask, "What about your theater? Why would you need to go back to *una vida peligrosa?*"

He looked at her patiently. "Most likely, *querida*, I will not have to. But the business of show has its ups and downs. We cannot rule out the need to raise capital in the future."

She frowned, confused. "*Que es* capital?"

"Money, child. 'If money go before, all ways do lie open.' "

"I *like* money," she said reasonably. "But killing? I do not like so much. I am a good Catholic girl."

"Yes, you are, my sweet. Finish your food before it gets cold."

"Bard says this?"

"No, Hargrave does."

She shrugged, hunkered back over the plate and shoveled eggs into her.

York said, "All of this thieving is to build your own theater? Did I get that right?"

Hargrave nodded, pushed his plate aside, then drank some coffee.

York frowned. "How can the notorious leader of the Hargrave gang be out in the open like that? You don't think Caleb York would track you down?"

"Not to Canada," he said, smiled tight, and drank some more coffee. "Perhaps you might find that part of the world to *your* liking, as well, Bret. A theater needs more than one man to run it."

And that was all the actor had to say on the subject.

York rose from the table. "I'll go up and get your guests and stick them in the parlor. All right? With me gone, someone else will have to look after them."

Hargrave shrugged. "Fetch them down for breakfast. A well-fed guest is a happy guest."

When York exited the hotel, the Indian was again sitting cross-legged by the double doors. The little Apache with the red turban and blue jacket had a way of glaring without putting any expression on his face. He did that now, but York ignored him and his glare.

In a few minutes, York returned, walking the gelding— all saddled-up and ready—back to the Inn. The outlaws' horses were hitched to the left. The buckboard with dead Ned Clutter in back in his wicker coffin was still tied up at the right, horse and all. The trotter had been denied the hay and the comforts of the livery stable. The sun was warmer today, so the flies were thicker.

Hargrave was waiting at the foot of the handful of steps up to the hotel porch.

York told him, "I'll get back here as fast as I can. If I'm not back in two days, you may want to find somewhere else to be. Some other state, maybe."

The actor's rueful laugh was barely audible. "You're probably right. By then Caleb York might find us, if we wear out our welcome here in Hell Junction."

"He might."

The outlaw held out his hand.

York took it, shook it.

"I'm full of fancy talk, Bret," Hargrave said, his smile vaguely embarrassed. "But as the Bard says, 'Words are easy, like the wind—faithful friends are hard to find.'"

Harder than you think, York thought, as he smiled back at the man, nodded, and climbed up onto the horse.

The ride out of Hell Junction was up a slope between two rocky hillsides, the one at his left rising and building into the mountain that once had given up enough silver to encourage the growth of a town, then been stingy enough to snuff it out. When the slope crested and leveled, before its gradual descent to the rocky area where yesterday York had faced three roads into these hills and mountains, he had a wooded area off to his right, beyond which was another rocky hill.

He had left town at a fast pace, but soon slowed the gelding to a gentle trot, having no intention of getting very far out of the ghost town before making his way back, to cut behind Main Street in back of the livery stable and the general store and the rest of the dead buildings. He sensed something and paused. Looked behind him and listened.

A pony was coming.

The hoofbeats told him as much, their lightness and how closely spaced they were. His smile had knowingness but little else in it, as he eased off the hard dirt road through the brush and into the trees, pulling up enough on the gelding's reins to stop the animal, which he then walked into the woods aways. He tied it up on a small but sturdy tree.

He listened sharp.

The pony was still coming.

Which meant Hargrave had sent someone to quietly shadow him. The outlaw actor may have considered McCory a friend, but that did not mean Hargrave trusted him entirely. York, who already knew who'd been sent, made his way through the trees and brush, leaves whispering as he pushed back through to his left, to a spot where some rocks edged the road. There he crouched and waited, .44 in hand.

Broken Knife, on a small pinto, its coat patchy with brown and white, was making his steady way in his task of secret chaperone. Suddenly the Apache in the cavalry jacket frowned and pulled up on his reins, stopping the pony. Both rider and horse went still as a statue.

The Apache's back was to York, who hid perhaps ten feet away. The little man's head was raised, as his ears took in every sound. York made none. Then the Indian's eyes traveled to the right, landing where York had left the road.

The Apache hopped off of the pony. From a sheath on his right hip he drew a big nasty-looking Bowie knife— the blade was long, nine inches anyway, and a good two inches wide; the wooden handle, walnut likely, had no guard. Crouching, making himself even smaller, the Apache held the Bowie tight in his sideways fist and crept toward the brush and the trees beyond.

York would have preferred to shoot the Indian and end this now. But they were still close enough to town that a shot might carry. Maybe he could take the Apache prisoner and leave him tied up in the woods, and slap the pony's rump and hope it headed for somewhere else.

York came out from behind the rock and, with less than ten feet separating them, told the Apache's back, "Drop the knife, amigo. Hands up."

The little man moved quicker than York had ever seen a human do, whipping around and throwing the blade at him, its whir carving the air.

But York was fast himself, batting the Bowie away with the .44 barrel, the steel of gun and knife clanging, and then the Indian was barreling toward him, like a charging animal, which is what he was, really, and when Broken Knife was almost on top of him, York slapped him alongside the face with the .44 barrel, hard.

The Indian, cheek slashed and bleeding, went down on the hard road surface, but was automatically pushing back up. Damnit, York didn't want a gunshot ripping a hole in the morning, though ripping a hole in this savage he wouldn't have minded. That hesitation on York's part was just enough for the Indian to tackle him, taking him down, and York's wrist hit a stone and the .44 went flying.

Then the Indian was on top of him, holding him down with a knee on the chest, the little man's hands gripped as if in frantic prayer, lifting them high over his head to bring down on York's face, a blow that the lawman knew would send the bones of his nose crashing into his brain and bringing on permanent darkness.

But in that fraction of a second, steel winked sunshine at him and from the corner of his eye he saw the Bowie knife waiting for someone to use it.

York did, grabbing the knife and shoving its blade deep into the little Apache's side. The attacker straightened and his eyes opened wide with the knowledge that death was coming.

Withdrawing the blade, York bucked the smaller man off.

Wounded and hurting, Broken Knife nonetheless was getting to his feet when York said to himself, *We're not having that*, and slipped behind the Apache and slit his throat, blood spraying the road and its rocky edge a glittering red, sunlight dancing on the scarlet wetness.

The geyser only lasted a few seconds, just long enough for the Apache's heart to stop pumping and its owner to flop face forward onto the dirt.

York dragged the carcass off the road into the brush. Nothing could be done about the bloody roadside, but none of the outlaws were likely to see it, between now and what York had ahead of him.

The pinto, which wore a blanket, not a saddle, was stirring but not going anywhere. York slapped its backside, saying, "*Yah! Yah!*" and off it went, heading away from Hell Junction.

Lucky pinto.

He collected the .44, checked it over, finding nothing jarred or dented that might compromise the action. Finding the buckskin jacket confining, he pitched it into the woods, not caring that Parker's ransom note went with it. Then he pushed through brush to the gelding and untied it. He climbed on and guided the animal to the road. The blood soaked in the dirt already was looking more black than red.

Heading back to Hell Junction at a trot, York worked at calming himself, slowing his breathing. Even Caleb York could get worked up and winded, dancing with a damn Indian wielding an Arkansas toothpick.

York was calm by the time he reached the dead city's outskirts, and he guided the gelding off the road and brought it and himself up behind the buildings. He cut over to the street that bordered Main and headed for the livery stable. Once there, he dismounted and walked the gelding to the barn-style rear doors.

Sounds were coming from within—horses whinnying some and moving in place, the stagecoach's lines and leaders and their metal work jangling. He expected this, but he drew the .44 nonetheless.

He went quickly in.

Jonathan Tulley, standing near the stagecoach, jumped in place and swung the scattergun toward York, who said, "Save it for the Hargrave bunch."

Tulley frowned. "You look a mite messed up, Caleb York."

"I had to kill an Indian."

The deputy frowned. "They ain't hostiles afoot, is they?" Then it came to him. "Oh! That Broken Knife feller."

"Yeah. Him."

"Ain't he suppose to've survived the Little Big Horn?"

"So I'm told."

Tulley cackled. "Well, he didn't survive no ruckus with Caleb York, did he?"

"He did not. But right now I'm more concerned with Caleb York surviving a ruckus with the Hargrave gang."

Tulley's expression grew serious. "So when do we go?"

"We go right now."

York checked Tulley's work. The four Morgan horses were hitched up to the stagecoach just as they should be. York was pleasantly surprised. The stagecoach had been led into the livery stable, nose first; somehow Tulley had turned the vehicle around, before hitching up the Morgans, so that the coach and the animals were facing the street.

"Tulley, how did you manage this? There's not room in here to swing the coach around. What did you do, drag it out the back?"

"Yessir."

"But it must weigh a ton. How the hell—"

"She's got wheels, ain't she?"

He decided to leave it at that.

But this was good, because York had assumed they would have to exit the back and come around to Main by way of the adjacent street. This would be better. More sudden, and some speed could be worked up, whereas what he'd assumed they'd be doing would have required two turns, which would really slow the coach and the animals down.

"Tulley, you need help getting up on the box?" The "box" was the stagecoach driver's seat.

"Hell no! Iffen I can turn this buggy aroun' my own seff, I surely can get my tail up on the gol-durn thing!"

And the former desert rat did just that. It was a little like watching a squirrel climb a tree.

York tied the gelding onto the back of the coach. Tulley's mule, Gert, was in a stall. She'd have to stay behind for now.

The deputy, shotgun in his lap, got the reins in hand. He looked down at a slightly astounded Caleb York and said, " 'Fraid I ain't gonna be much help where shootin' is concerned. Got my hands full with these reins and horses."

"I know. Shooting is my lookout. You know how those brakes work?"

"Shore do. Ready when you are, Sheriff."

"You're a good man, Jonathan Tulley. Did I ever tell you that?"

"Once or twict."

York opened the front doors, and Tulley told the horses, "*Git up! Git up!*"

And he, and they, got.

But Tulley held back on the reins some. The coach was not to get up to full speed. Not yet.

Stagecoach and driver rumbled out of the livery stable, and York—.44 in hand—tucked behind the coach and ran along with it, holding on at the rear boot, with the gelding keeping pace.

The coach swung left and headed for the hotel.

They had a pick-up to make.

CHAPTER FOURTEEN

Several minutes before Caleb York and Jonathan Tulley began their short stagecoach ride from the livery stable to the Hell Junction Inn, Willa Cullen was inside the hotel, sitting with Rita Filley on the two-seater sofa by the boarded-up windows onto the street. To the right of the women, in the chair where he'd first been deposited in the parlor the day before, was Raymond Parker.

To Willa's left, in a chair pulled over from a wall, sat a rumpled, frazzled-looking Doc Miller, who earlier had escorted Ben Bemis, the wounded gang member, into the dining salon for a parlay among the outlaws. Across from them, the glass-and-wood doors stood open to the dining room, where Hargrave was at the table closest to those open doors—possibly to better keep an eye on the hostages. Seated with him were Reese Randabaugh, Bemis, and the Mexican woman, Juanita.

A forlorn-looking Randy Randabaugh was at the next table, alone, sitting there slumped, in the same gray shirt with arm garters he'd worn flagging down the stage just yesterday, seeming a much nicer boy than he'd proved to be. The Wileys were either not invited to the party or were choosing to be somewhere else. Tension, after all, was running high.

Bemis—the burly, bushy-bearded individual in a plaid jacket who at the holdup had struck Willa as resembling a miner—looked pale and seemed sluggish, either from pain or the doctor's pills. He was saying little. Of course, their leader held center stage, doing most of the talking.

"I anticipate," the actor was saying, "that Mr. McCory will be back with our due rewards no later than late tomorrow afternoon. He will have with him a business associate of Mr. Parker's, who will make the exchange. It's highly likely that this business associate will be accompanied by a Pink or some other bodyguard. But that's of no matter."

Reese had been squinting skeptically at his boss through all of that. "It *isn't?*"

Hargrave shook his head. "I have no intention of allowing this exchange to be anything *but* a peaceful one."

The older Randabaugh leaned forward, hands pressed against the linen-covered table top, halfway out of his seat. "You're going to let him *go?*"

The outlaw leader flipped a hand. "I'm going to set all of them free. It's simply good business."

Juanita was on her feet and swearing at him in Spanish, teeth bared, eyes flaring, spittle flying.

Reese glanced in the direction of the hostages in the parlor and got up, closing the doors on them.

Willa did not hear the ensuing conversation, though the animated expressions of all concerned—but for the composed, self-contained Hargrave—spoke volumes.

What she'd have heard would have chilled her.

Juanita said, "These are *witnesses!* There were *killings!* Their *testimonio* will hang us!"

Hargrave gestured graciously for his paramour to sit back down. She didn't. She just folded her arms on the shelf of her bosom and glared at her man.

Who said, "We will be long gone, *querida*, in a place where we can't be touched. Do not worry your pretty self."

Her teeth were bared, her head back. "You are *sweet* on that *perra rubia!* You *lust* for her!"

He didn't allow himself to be drawn into her storm. "I am not, and I do not. I am kind to her only to keep her calm and manageable."

"Never mind that blonde bitch," Reese said, accidentally translating Juanita's epithet. "What I want to know is, why do you trust a damn *stranger* like this McCory? What's to keep him from takin' the ransom money and hightailin'?"

"That won't happen," Hargrave said, waving that off. "Parker's people won't hand across that kind of money anywhere *but* the exchange. And we will be in the rocks watching as that takes place."

Looking as if he were on the verge of passing out, Bemis said, "I don't like it. I get damn near shot to death, and some *outsider* is part of the gang now? Trusted with gettin' our damn *money* for us? All due respect, Mr. Hargrave, this don't seem right *a* tall."

Hargrave patted the air with a palm. "No need for these qualms, gentlemen. I have dispatched our friend Broken Knife to shadow Mr. McCory, to make certain he does our bidding."

The conversation ended there, because Hargrave and the others heard what Willa now heard, though a few seconds after she did: *the jangle of stagecoach ribbons and the hoofbeats of its horses.*

But then she'd been waiting for that. So had Parker, Rita, and Doc.

The gang had done them a favor, congregating in the dining room like that. Had the outlaws been in the parlor, the hostages would have had to wait until the fuss started and hope to slip out the back way, with the outlaws' attention drawn elsewhere.

But this arrangement allowed Willa and the others— Doc Miller in the lead, closest to the double doors onto the street—to make their escape as the horses and the vehicle they bore came to a sudden whinnying halt. Jonathan Tulley, up in the box, shotgun in his lap, had yanked the brake lever with one hand and with the other pulled the reins to a stop. Within seconds, the captives were outside, on the porch, then clambering down the steps and up into the waiting stagecoach, Parker holding the door for them as first Willa, then Rita, piled in, followed quickly by Doc Miller and Parker himself.

Willa glimpsed Caleb York at the rear of the coach, behind his dappled-gray, black-maned gelding tied onto the boot. He flashed her a tight smile, but his eyes were on the hotel, whose broken-out but boarded-up windows allowed slots for weapons from within to be wielded.

Then, with the former hostages barely in their seats, the coach took off, Tulley yelling, "*Yee-haw! Yee-haw!*"

And the jangle of reins and hoofbeats of horses picked up again, almost as if they had never stopped, and the stagecoach, the gelding tied behind it, charged down Main Street, leaving behind a dust cloud . . .

. . . and Caleb York.

Blaine Hargrave was the first one out of the dining room and into the parlor, fast on his feet but not enough so to get there before the front doors, with their fancy stained-glass windows, swung themselves shut behind the fleeing hostages.

And by the time Hargrave got to a front window in the parlor, his knees on a sofa still warm from Willa Cullen's backside, he saw only the stagecoach rumbling off and the cloud of dust that subsumed a male figure that, of all people, appeared to be Bret McCory.

Reese rushed to the two-seater sofa, and his knees found the warmth Rita Finney had left behind. He was at the window, too, muttering, "*McCory? What the hell . . . ?*"

Then, as the dust dissipated, no one was there.

Hargrave called out: "What have you *done*, man? *Et tu*, Bret?"

Young Randy was behind them, a .45 in hand. "Who et what?"

Hargrave spat, "Take a window, man!"

Reese did, shoving aside the chair that had been Parker's to get at it.

"*The name's Caleb York!*" came the familiar voice from somewhere in or across the street. "*Never saw this Bret McCory in my life—and neither have you!*"

Juanita was leaning in beside Hargrave, putting a hand on his shoulder. "How can I help, *querida*?"

"Seems someone in our little play was a better actor than I," he told her with a rueful smile. "I've been up-staged."

"What can I *do*?"

Then he looked hard at her and said, "You can start by going upstairs and getting your thirty-eight."

She nodded and ran off through the lobby and up the stairs.

Bemis, looking barely able to stay conscious, stood in the parlor waiting for directions.

From outside thundered that voice again: *"I'm sheriff of Trinidad County, and you're all under arrest! Throw out your weapons and come out with your hands empty and high!"*

Hargrave said, "There's only one of him and five of us. So we wait him out. In the meantime, Broken Knife will sneak up on him like a good little redskin and get rid of the white eyes."

As if he'd heard that, York yelled: *"Get out here now, or I will cut you down like I did your Indian scout! Your choice."*

Hargrave could see no target, and no shots had been leveled their way; nothing provided help in figuring the sheriff's position . . .

Still on his knees on the sofa, the outlaw leader said, "All right, everyone. We can't get to the horses, either out front or in the stable. We have no choice but to go out the back way and come around and flank the bastard."

Bemis said, "I ain't much on runnin' and gunnin' at present. How about I take a high winder?"

"Do that," Hargrave said, nodding as he got off the couch and onto his feet. "Reese, you and your brother go out by the kitchen. You go left, Reese, and Randy, go right. Head down behind a building or two and squeeze our friend between you."

"Whatever you say, Blaine," Reese said. Smiling, eyes glittering, the older Randabaugh obviously relished the idea that his competition for Hargrave's approval would soon be removed from the gang—and that he might be the one doing the removing, was all the sweeter . . .

Randy, so hangdog this morning from last night's trashing and humiliation, had come alive, the blond boy smiling and holding his .45 with its barrel in the air, as if about to fire the starting shot on a race.

And it *was* a race of sorts—which of them could get to York first without getting themselves killed . . .

But Hargrave had something else in mind for himself and Juanita. Muttering, he said, "Son of a bitch always did have a lean and hungry look . . ."

Reese frowned. "What, Blaine?"

"Nothing. Get to it. Enjoy yourselves. Surviving this is the prize now, because our hostages are lost to us."

Caleb York was positioned behind Doc Miller's buckboard, which remained tied to the hotel's façade. The outlaws within hadn't seemed to get a fix on him yet, and not a single shot had been fired his way, though he'd seen the barrels of revolvers poking from between the slats of the boarded-up windows.

That the gang would stay inside and use the hotel as their fortress remained a possibility, but York considered it a distant one. Managing to keep them pinned down might give Doc Miller time to raise a posse to send to support him. But that would be hours from now.

He'd considered having Tulley drive the stage a respectable distance and then let either Doc Miller or Raymond Parker take over at the reins, delivering the women back to Trinidad. That would have given him Tulley and his scattergun, making it possible to keep both the front and back of the hotel covered.

But getting those two females back to safety had been his major concern, and he didn't feel confident that either Miller or Parker could handle the role of stagecoach driver.

So that left him here, a man alone, which was probably his preference anyway. He grinned as he peeked around the rear of the buckboard. Ned Clutter was getting ripe, but at least the ruckus had scared the flies off.

Now several minutes had gone by and nothing—not a voice, not a gunshot—had emanated from the hotel, the slots between boards on those windows no longer sprouting gun barrels, either.

So they were coming for him.

He felt his best bet, in that case, was to hug the buildings along the boardwalk of the ghost town, though the squeaks of the weathered wood underfoot, and the spurs on his boots, would almost certainly announce him. Keeping a gun in his right hand, he sat on the crushed-rock street behind the buckboard, and his left hand encouraged his boots off. In his stocking feet now, he could edge down that boardwalk and not be easily heard, as long as he took care.

Staying low, he started around the buckboard, at his left, but this exposed him in the street briefly, which was enough to draw a shot from above.

York ducked, rolled, and aimed up at a vague figure in a second-floor window. The .44 cracked the silence and the window glass. The vague figure seemed to totter, as if the man were using his last conscious moments on earth to decide whether to fall backward or forward.

The shooter chose the latter and burst through the window in a shower of shards and crunching glass and splintered wood, pitching onto the overhang of the hotel porch. He rolled like a log down and off that roof and hit the street with a *whump*, raising dust.

By this time York was under that overhang, his back against the building. Wondering who he'd killed, York looked past the still hitched-up horses of the outlaws at the facedown bearded man in the street, and figured this to be Ben Bemis, who he'd never seen before. That was as much thought as he gave that subject, as staying alive was more important.

So he crept along the boardwalk, past the next building, what had been a laundry, waiting for someone to try to come around on him from the back. With spaces between buildings, he needed to glance behind him every two seconds or so. His progress was slow.

Then, between a dead restaurant and the equally defunct post office, Reese Randabaugh emerged onto the boardwalk, gun in hand raised and ready to shoot, just a few feet from York. The older Randabaugh's face contorted with rage, his hatred and perhaps his jealousy of the man who'd called himself Bret McCory overwhelming him for half a second.

York, not encumbered with any such emotion, used that half second to blow a hole through Reese's forehead. The close-set eyes, shared by the brothers, had just time to widen before the works within him shut off; the hole, not quite in the center of his brow, looked black, then wept a single scarlet tear that trickled between blue eyes.

Then Reese tumbled to the boardwalk, his head hanging off the slightly elevated side, leaking blood and brain and bone matter onto the crushed-rock street.

York headed back the way he came, figuring they would try a pincer move, meaning the next gun should come from the other side of the hotel, between it and the assay office. As York moved by Doc's hitched-up buckboard, the trotter restlessly dancing after the gunfire, he wondered if he'd misjudged their strategy; but then

Randy Randabaugh stepped out from between buildings, revolver ready, and looked past York at his fallen brother. Screaming, the boy started shooting wildly, staying put but issuing one gunshot after another. The idiocy of this non-tactic caught York by surprise. He dove into the street, seeking to return fire from a prone position.

Randy had availed himself of a second handgun and was firing just as wildly with it now, pausing only to skirt Doc's buckboard, making it momentarily impossible for York to return fire. When the boy was in view, in the street, the incessant gunfire caused York to have to again roll back out of the way.

"*Randy!*" a female voice called.

The blond boy froze and his eyes went to the source, a female figure in the window, the same one where Ben Bemis died; framed in the broken-glass teeth, she stood holding a double-barreled shotgun, its twin black bottomless eyes aimed down.

Mahalia either had experience with such a weapon or was just plain lucky. The first barrel turned the boy's groin into a bloody mess. His mouth opened but nothing came out, as if screaming just didn't cover his loss. The second barrel took his head off. Blood shot up like an oil well coming in. But the gusher was brief.

York got to his feet and smiled up at the girl. She was smiling, too. He tipped his hat to her and moved on.

This left only Hargrave and Juanita. York figured the woman was at least as dangerous as the man, unless they both had covered their tails by siccing the Randabaughs and Bemis on him while they quietly left out a backstage door.

No, he thought. *He had ruined enough things for Har-*

grave and his honey to keep them here seeking revenge.
Hamlet was the actor's most famous role, after all. . . .

York walked past the Buckhorn Saloon, its broken
window saying only BUC and OON now. Next door was
the Palace Theater, where Hargrave had likely once performed; its façade had no windows at all, just the bold
lettering announcing itself and a marquee to add who
was playing. No one, right now. Unless . . .

Surely the actor would not take refuge *there*, of all
places!

But actors, particularly Shakespearean ones, had a
love of poetry, and of the inherently dramatic gesture,
and what more dramatic, poetic place could there be for
the last confrontation between archenemies than the
ghost town's playhouse?

And, indeed, the front doors of the Palace Theater
stood open. Someone—well, there were only two possibilities—had engaged the wedges that had once upon a
time been used to keep those doors open to the public.

York, .44 in hand, slowly entered the small foyer. A
box-office booth, its gilded cage festooned with spider-
webs, was to the right. Staying close to the wall, York
crept over there, to see if Hargrave or the woman might
be within, waiting to jack-in-the-box up and hand him,
on the house, a ticket to hell.

But no.

The space within was empty, home only to more spi-
ders and their webs.

The two inner doors were also wedged open. Hargrave
was staging the production with some care, considering
the lack of time available. York stepped inside, under a
balcony's overhang. The chamber seemed vast, though
the structure itself was not elaborate, just a wooden husk

whose red and gold decorative paint was blistered where it wasn't gone. Several box seats on either side overlooked the stage, whose frayed curtains, open to expose an empty, dusty proscenium, seemed to be hanging on for dear life.

No seats in this theater. Likely the space had been used for dances as well as plays and musical events, so folding chairs that could be cleared when necessary had provided seating. What had become of them was lost to the ages, as if anyone cared.

York stepped out from under the balcony, listening for any sign of either of them. Glanced up there and saw nothing. Perhaps they had led him here in order to come up on him from behind. But he heard nothing.

Then came applause—the sound of one person clapping.

It rang through the high-ceilinged room, echoing, as if it were announcing the star of this performance.

Which it was.

Blaine Hargrave, in his customary black, stepped from the wings and kept clapping till he reached center stage. His jacket was back to reveal the revolver on his hip, low and tied-down. Was that the show the outlaw planned? To shoot it out with his Brutus?

"It's what I get," Hargrave said, his voice carrying without trying too hard, "for wearing my heart on my sleeve."

"More like hoist on your own petard."

Hargrave gestured with his left hand, perhaps realizing a movement of his right, near his weapon, could get him killed. He said, "'The fault, dear Brutus, is not in our stars . . .'"

"That's enough of this bull," York said. "Unbuckle that gun belt and let it drop. I'm taking you to Trinidad. Your next performance is in front of the circuit judge. Anything clever or Shakespearean to say about that?"

The actor, alone on his stage, shook his head. "No. I prefer to save my farewell speech for the gallows."

Some particles of dirt drifted down and landed on York's shoulder. He hurled himself out onto the dusty floor, looking up to see just who he expected: Juanita—at the rail of the balcony, with a revolver in her hand and hatred on her pretty face. She was trying to draw a bead on York when he shot her, the angle of the bullet starting under a cheek and traveling out the top of the back of her head, a spray of red blossoming like a beautiful, terrible flower that wilted at once.

The shot took her backward and she slipped out of sight just as she slipped out of life. The scream from the stage told York that he best roll to one side and face that direction. There he saw Hargrave leaping, revolver in hand, handsome face contorted into agonized ugliness, jumping from the stage much as he'd done when that heckler taunted him and sent him down a torturous path that was ending here.

Hargrave was still in the air when York's bullet lanced through him, in the chest, and when he hit the floor, it was with no grace at all.

The gun had fled the actor's fingers, but even if it hadn't, the man was so close to death that when York approached him, no danger awaited. The lawman knelt over the outlaw.

Hargrave, sprawled on his back, was smiling. At first York thought the man was looking at him, but no—the actor was looking *through* York.

Then the dying man said, weakly but with perfect enunciation despite a bubbling mouthful of blood, " 'Juliet, I will lie with thee tonight.' "

York stood, wondering if that was from the balcony scene.

Sure seemed like it should have been.

CHAPTER FIFTEEN

Gun in hand, not sure of what or who he'd find, York checked the hotel, top to bottom, though as far as he knew those presenting any real problem were nicely deceased. But he was in particular looking to see what had become of the Wileys, who were surely still breathing.

Their well-appointed living quarters, in which York had previously not set foot, evidenced signs of a quick departure—dresser drawers open and empty or nearly so, a wardrobe with perhaps a third of the clothing missing and the rest in disarray. It would seem they had used the melee to provide cover for a back-door escape.

That made sense, as now that the sheriff of Trinidad County knew of the Hell Junction Inn's existence, its value to the outlaw world would be nil. York had already determined to shut the place down.

The colored servant, Mahalia, he found in her room off the kitchen, where she sat on the edge of the cot, looking entirely self-composed. She was neatly dressed in a dark blue calico winter day dress that must have been what she wore to church.

Maybe that was why York instinctively took off his hat when he spoke to her. "Are you all right, miss?"

"You a lawman."

"I am."

"You gon' take me to the pokey?"

He went over and sat next to her, his hat in his hands and in his lap. His smile was gentle. "I'd sooner throw you a dinner in your honor at a real hotel," he said.

"I killed a man."

"Not much of one. You saved my life."

Her eyes were big and dark and locking on his. "You saved *me* last night."

That embarrassed him. "Do you have something you could gather your things in?"

"Pillow case?"

"The Wileys seem to have vacated their quarters."

"I heard them scurry. Thought they might collect me. They didn't."

"Why don't you go over to their quarters and see if they left behind a carpetbag or such? If they did, fill it and come out front and wait."

She nodded. He patted her shoulder, and went out.

The hotel was otherwise empty. He collected his own things, including his saddlebags, then walked over to the livery. He noticed two horses that had been stabled there were gone—probably the Wileys' own animals. But two of four horses that had been the outlaws', hitched in front of the hotel, were also gone. The couple had likely commandeered them as pack animals to take as many of their belongings as they could quickly assemble.

However you cut it, the innkeepers had skedaddled—guests who were running out on their bill. York didn't much care. He'd put a stop to their business of providing a hideout with clean sheets and indoor privies for the likes of the Hargrave bunch, and that was good enough for him.

Tulley's mule, Gert, had a stall. So that made four animals to lead back to Trinidad. If that servant girl could drive a buckboard, he could ride along on his gelding with Gert behind him and two horses behind the wagon. That would spare him a trip back to this place. He would see.

For now the hardest part of this damn day lay ahead: gathering the dead. He could have left them to feed the critters and take their own good time turning to skeletons. But he felt he owed it to the men he'd killed—and the woman—to haul them back to civilization.

Anyway, he was pretty sure he had wanted posters on Bemis and the Randabaughs, and there were places outside the territory where Hargrave was worth at least a thousand, dead or alive. Corpses could be shipped, after all. Worth a try. A sheriff depended on such rewards to supplement his somewhat meager pay.

And so Caleb York began dragging the bodies from where they fell, the blood fresh enough to leave snail-like trails. He reunited the Hargrave gang, piling the bodies like cordwood in the back of the buckboard, having to stack Hargrave himself on top of Clutter's wicker coffin, which crunched some from that.

The worst was the woman.

Well, not the worst—the headless Randy Randabaugh was not pleasant to view, though York didn't mind not seeing that stupid face with its close-set eyes again. But the woman? Caleb York had never killed a woman before, and felt a mite bad about it.

He rested her, facedown, on top of Hargrave, face up, figuring that's how they'd want it, though the nasty exit wound on the top of her head made him twitch a frown. He covered their final embrace with the tarp. Piling them up like that had invited a war party of flies that he'd been batting away at, getting bit a few times.

Nasty work. Nastier than killing them.

The back of the buckboard was stacked so high with the dead that he wouldn't bother stopping on the road to add Broken Knife to his collection. He didn't know of any warrants out on the Apache, and anyway, many people in this part of the world still didn't value Indians much alive, let alone dead.

But York knew Broken Knife had been the toughest, hardest man he'd fought today, and he respected that.

Mahalia watched much of this from the porch, standing with a small carpetbag in her two hands, held primly in front of her. If she was troubled or sickened by the sight of him hauling dead bodies and loading them up in a wagon like bags of grain, she did not show it.

When he was done, York was sweating and worn out. Dealing with dead men was harder than handling living ones. He fanned his face with the battered gray Stetson and looked up at her from the bottom of the stairs.

"You ever drive a buckboard, miss?"

"I done it for the Wileys afore."

He snugged on the Stetson. "Good. If you have a hanky you can tear, you might stuff some strips up your nostrils. That'll cut the stench. Some of these freshly dead soiled themselves dyin', and there's one from yesterday going ripe already."

"I'll do that. Sheriff York?"

"Yes, miss?"

"You really not taking me to jail?"

"No, miss."

"Where *are* you takin' me?"

"The town of Trinidad will pay for a ticket on the stage to Las Vegas, and a train ticket from there to anywhere you like."

"They do that?"

"When you save the sheriff's life, they do. But I think Miss Filley—Rita—can find something for you at the Victory Saloon. She'll help you with a room, too. Or Miss Cullen might have something at her ranch."

She licked her lips. "You're awful good to me, sir. How can I repay you?"

She was a lovely thing, but he already had one woman too many. So he simply said, "Just help me get the dead back to town. I know an undertaker who is going to be a real happy man today."

Despite the weighted-down load, the girl did well with the buckboard. York rode alongside her, with a mule tied behind him and two horses trailing the load of corpses. When they got to the narrow road out of Hale Junction, he would move up and lead the way.

For now, they rode out of the ghost town, buckboard rumbling, York and his gelding loping along. The Main Street was so like Trinidad, with only the faded façades and blistered paint and weathered wood to say the municipality was no more. He wondered if maybe he shouldn't burn this place down—the hotel anyway. One lit match would do the trick.

But it just didn't seem right, somehow.

Not right at all, burning down a ghost town when it just acquired so many new residents.